# DEDICATION

**Sylvester Stallone**
My biggest idol, role model and inspiration in life.

# ACKNOWLEDGEMENTS

Mum, Steve, Dad, and Bro for all the support.

Jake Best for allowing me to use the cover image but most importantly coming into my life and showing me true beast-mode when I needed it the most.

Eoin Friel CEO @ The Action Elite
(theactionelite.com)

&
ORV Photography for the cover image
(orvphotography.com)

# The Devil...

*Fight Night spectacle.*
*London's O2 Arena.*
*Full house.*

Logan "The Devil" Devlin – six-feet-four, built like a tank, and in his prime, fought hammer-and-tong with the one and only British champion Anthony Joshua when the tapping sound ringside rung out to indicate ten-seconds remaining of the round.

The Sky Sports commentators, Adam Smith and Johnny Nelson, sat glued to the edge of their seats, both like wide-eyed children in anticipation to the developing fight.

'Final ten seconds of round six, and The Devil is standing his ground well with Joshua!' Adam was shouting to Johnny. Even sitting at his side, he could hardly be heard over the chanting of the crowd.

'Josh-ua—Josh-ua—Josh-ua—'

Logan ducked a killer punch, countering with a brutal right hook square on Joshua's jaw.

The crack of bone on bone broke through the chants. Joshua crashed to the canvas and stirred on his back.

'AJ is down!' screamed Johnny with a broken voice.

Adam exclaimed, 'I don't believe it!'

A buzz filled the ring as the entire arena stood stunned, filled with disappointment for seeing their dearest favourite stirring on his back as the referee begun the count. 'And for only the second time in Joshua's career, he is down!' Would he get back up? Could he get back up?

Johnny scanned the arena. 'The entire London O2 Arena is on its feet.' They were all waiting.

The bell rung, breaking the stunned silence and ending the round.

'Saved by the bell. What a right hook from The Devil.'

Smiling through his black gum-shield at his tank-like coach, Buck, and Buck's skinny, knowledgeable assistant, Larry, both in their forties, Logan headed to his corner. He winked to his black haired beauty, Faith Jenkins, who was sitting nervously on edge ringside. She sat, all alone, with no makeup on and far too underdressed for such an event. A faint green bruise stained her pale face, like the bruise on an apple, ruining such beauty. She nervously fiddled her engagement ring and smiled a broken smile up at her poised warrior as he waltzed smugly to his stool.

Behind Logan, Joshua rose on wobbly legs with the referee scrutinising him before giving the all-clear to return to his dismayed corner.

Joshua's corner sat him on the stool and frantically tended to him. The advice from each corner couldn't have been more different. Logan's was more of the same onslaught, whilst Joshua's was to recover and counter The Devil's onslaught and to try and return fire with the jab.

The bell rung for time; the two fighters rose off their stools with guards raised and ready to fight.

'Into the eighth round,' announced Adam.

Joshua hadn't even time to settle into the round before Logan had him against the ropes, unleashing swift, powerful combos to body and face — a killing machine — finishing with a solid right uppercut. Sweat sprayed off Joshua's hair as he hit the canvas for now the third time in his career. The crowd was further dismayed.

'He's down — he's down again!' roared Adam.

'AJ is down and doesn't know what day of the week it is!' affirmed Johnny. The referee waved his arms to the judges ringside — fight over.

'It's over! The referee has called the fight and Logan 'The Devil' Devlin is the new WBC Heavyweight Champion!' cried Adam, wiping the sweat from his flustered face.

'I don't believe it. I really don't, and nor can the crowd,' declared Johnny.

Joshua's coach and assistant leapt through the ropes to his aid, along with the medics, as the referee sat the disorientated Joshua up.

'This man is an animal.'

'I know, Adam. I mean is there anyone out there who could go the distance with The Devil? Let alone defeat him...?'

'I don't think so, Johnny. Even God himself would have trouble against The Devil...'

# ...The Saviour

Days later, on a wintry night, a white butterfly fluttered over the misty harbour of Poole Quay, Dorset. A modern-day ship's foghorn sounded out through the darkness. The butterfly wandered over the traditional quayside pubs spanning across this old pirate's haven and over the jingling masts of docked boats before descending towards a picturesque Georgian building with a regal sweeping staircase which led to happy diners bestowed with such a sea view. This was the old Custom House, now converted to an a-la-carte restaurant upstairs and a cosy intimate café/bar below. The butterfly continued over a gate around the back, over empty beer kegs and industrial sized bins, until finally it rested on the kitchen window.

Inside the empty kitchen, Salvatore De Luca's brown soulless eyes stared into space as he mopped the floor. In his early thirties and his friends still called him Tory, it was clear that life hadn't been all that good to him. Or was it the other way round? But either way, his black scruffy beard and messy hair told the world that this man no longer really gave a damn. A bit shorter than most athletes, his body definition beneath his sweat-stained work clothes was evidence that this man once looked after himself.

It was eleven and a case of 'same shit, different shift'. With each tick of the mounted wall clock, the only thing that *really* changed was the water from his bucket getting murkier and murkier with each plunge of the mop. *How did it get to this?* he thought when the sight of the white butterfly resting outside on the small window pane brought it all back to light, reminding him of what he caused only years ago. Strangely, the more the butterfly 'stared' at him, the more the tragic memories resurfaced destroying his broken heart ever more so. Without thought, he simply made a fist, knuckles concealed by his cuffs, and swiftly punched the pane of glass in a vain attempt to send this elusive fluttering beauty on its way.

It worked; so the butterfly fluttered away but so did the single small window pane crack from one end to the other.

His soul-destroying flashbacks were soon interrupted when the two young-spirited chefs, Stewart and Robert, entered the kitchen excitedly with no regard for the nice clean floor.

'I can't believe we've just cooked for The Devil!' glowed Robert, the head chef to Stewart whilst grabbing his rucksack.

'I know, Bobby! Shit, what if he didn't like it?'

'We would've known about it by now.'

Tory glanced at the mucky footprints with his thousand-yard-stare and with a heavy plunge of the mop, he simply re-mopped over the messy prints.

Stewie spotted Tory and shadowboxed his way up to him with a beaming smile.

'Hey, Tory, like I tried asking earlier before we got rammed; you got any tips?'

Tory kept his eyes pinned down on the task at hand. It was safer for everyone. 'Wet floors can be slippery.'

'Ah, come on, man. I'm being serious. I mean for my white-collar charity fight I've just signed up to do.'

'Don't bother,' Tory muttered.

'Easy, Tiger, it's only a bit of fun.'

Tory snorted. 'Fun? Go fly a kite.'

'And it's for charity.'

'Charity? Put money in a box, a trust, foundation... something.'

'Ah, come on, be a sport, brother!'

Tory slowly peeled his eyes from the floor and threw a killer glare at Stewie.

'You're not my brother!'

'Okay—okay! Jees!'

Robert pulled Stewie away from pending danger.

'Told you he wouldn't, Stewie.'

The door swung open breaking the tension with a burst of noise from the restaurant, and the young, sweet barmaid, Bonnie, popped her head around the door. 'Um…The Devil-guy is kinda in the bar now taking autographs.'

Stewie and Robert's eyes lit up.

'Maybe he'll be kind enough to give you some tips,' said Robert to Stewie.

The two excitedly hurried out of the kitchen to meet the new champ.

*Could it be? The new British heavyweight champion is in here? Now?* thought Tory. *But why all the way down south, here in Dorset?* he pondered, and as he stepped forward to peer through the circular kitchen window and out into the bar area, the white butterfly caught his eye again, almost like it was watching him mop floors for a living. Tory shared this moment with this butterfly and with one deep anguished sigh, he looked down into his mucky bucket to find his pitiful, bearded face staring back at him. A final plunge of the mop distorted his reflection as he returned to kitchen-mopping duty, washing away any thoughts of boxing.

Tory couldn't hide in the kitchen forever to avoid all the action out in the bar. He signed out, pinned his pinny, and pulled his black hoody over his head. He stepped into the bar area avoiding contact while minding his own business and focusing on his hand exerciser.

A small group of customers, along with Stewie and Robert, congregated around The Devil who sat proudly on a leather sofa, taking selfies with fans and writing out autographs. He bared his golden grin. The rows of golden teeth in his mouth glinted, only adding to the sinister air of his demeanour. It was now Stewie and Robert's turn. They were crouched down low on either side of The Devil taking their picture with the champ.

When Tory entered the bar, he was still hammering away at his squeaky hand exerciser; his mind was fixated on the repetitious squeak. He wanted nothing to do with any of the fuss and simply wanted to get as far away from the boxing scene as possible.

Bonnie tried to stop Tory before he escaped through the noisy bar. 'They're all round that way,' said Bonnie to Tory, but he simply ignored her and continued round the opposite side of the narrow bar towards the staff room and fire exit. 'Beer?' Bonnie called out to Tory, doing anything in her power to keep the man she had the hots for to stay longer, but he simply focussed on the floor and shook his head. 'But you always…'

And just as he thought he had gotten away, divine intervention indeed intervened when Faith exited the toilets, brushing past Tory. As the two passed and touched, Faith uttered a quick apology under her breath at the hooded stranger, and in that very same instance Tory sniffed the sweet scent of perfume in the air and felt an overwhelming awareness course through his body—a sickly sensation in the deepest depths of his gut and with a skip of his broken heart's beating, his squeaky hand exerciser stopped. He shuddered and slowly turned around in awe to indeed find his gut-wrenching senses hadn't deceived him. Because right there, right in front of him, was Faith heading towards all the action. She was the only person who could have stopped Tory in his tracks from his sole mission to abandon ship and get as far away from this place as possible.

'Faith?'

She stopped in her tracks for a mere heartbeat before continuing into the bar. Faith knew exactly who it was calling her name; this was once their local hangout after all. Without looking back at Tory, she moved on but this time faster and with more conviction. A ship's foghorn sounded danger as Tory followed her. As if on autopilot, completely oblivious to his scruffy look and his reeking kitchen clothes, he moved towards the action he'd wished to avoid so very much in the first place.

'Faith! Faith, please!' continued Tory, following her like some puppy dog and completely oblivious to the fact that she was now Logan's girl. Logan had a fan's phone extended in one hand ready to take a group-selfie when he heard his girl's name being shouted by a *man*. He scanned the crowd for the offender with murderous eyes only to spot Tory, covered in kitchen shit, as he froze at the entrance to the bar.

Tory could only watch as Faith hurried back to Logan's side. Logan grinned his golden menacing smile at Tory. With a hefty push to the nearby fan, he slowly stood up ignoring the fan he just nearly plummeted head-first into the fireplace.

'You speakin' to *my* bitch?'

Tory's eyes remained transfixed on Faith. He didn't give a damn about Logan. Faith glanced at Tory, instinctively covering her faint bruise with her white fringe caused by severe trauma.

Logan kept his killer eyes fixated on Tory whilst snapping at Faith, 'Where's my JD?' Tory watched Faith pin her eyes down on the floor and hurry to the nearby bar just in front of Tory. Even in this intensifying moment, Tory remained aware of how beautiful she smelt; a smell he had never forgotten. What he couldn't believe though was how underdressed she was and how plain, yet still beautiful, her face was compared to when *he* knew her.

'Hey! I'm talkin' to you. Look at *me!*' snapped Logan whilst clicking his fingers to bring Tory round from his spellbound lustful moment.

Tory tore his stricken eyes from Faith and gazed up at The Devil.

'What you talkin' to her for?' Logan snarled, edging a step closer with an inquisitive look, when suddenly it clicked. 'Tory? That you under there? Shit the bed, it is, ain't it? Salvatore 'The Saviour' De Luca. You look like shit! Smell like it, too.'

Tory came back down to earth as the realisation struck him of the situation and his whereabouts. He was standing like a dick, having surfaced from the stinking depths of the kitchens to now be in front of a congregation of swanky customers all of whom were now fixated on him looking and smelling like shit.

Logan eyed Tory head to toe with disgust and continued his sole mission to belittle him more. 'You the cook? My dinner was cold.'

Bonnie was in the midst of pouring the Jack Daniels, and wanting to keep the peace, interrupted. 'Oh, he's just the dishwasher.' Logan erupted into laughter in Tory's face as Tory glanced at Faith with shame; his intense eyes causing her to fidget even though she wasn't going to look at him.

Logan's laughter stopped in a flash as his demeanour turned to spite and aggression. 'Then my plate was dirty.'

An awkward pause fell upon the bar as Bonnie asked Faith if she'd like a drink. Logan answered for her, grinning smugly at

Tory. 'Not for this one, she'll be no use to man or beast later…if you know what I mean.' Logan slapped her butt causing the drink to slosh in her hand before snatching it away.

Tory felt the fire ignite inside him and blood to rush his face at the sight of seeing Logan's monstrous hands touch Faith's butt. Bonnie, knowing Tory too well, passed him a pint regardless to extinguish any potential Italian fire getting out of hand.

Logan continued with his bullying and belittling tactics. 'Dishwasher? Really?' He laughed and checked to see if Faith was laughing along. Her acting skills weren't very good as she forced a chuckle while pinning her eyes on the bar, self-consciously hiding her faint bruise from Tory again with her white fringe.

'The Saviour. I never quite understood it. I mean, should be more like The Incapacitator, shouldn't it? After what you caused?'

Uh-oh.

Tory felt his heart race, his mouth run dry, and a lump form in his throat as a bagful of mixed emotions surfaced: rage, sorrow, grief. He swiped the pint and turned his back, taking a long swig.

'Did you hear?' continued Logan, 'I'm number one—the Champ. That's what you get for not being a quitter.' Tory remained intent on his drink. His silence only wound The Devil up even more. 'Oi, you listenin'? The cat got your tongue?' he slapped Faith's butt good and proper. 'I rule the roost now.'

The giant slap ricocheted through Tory like a bullet, but instead of breaking every bone in his body, it simply went straight for the heartbreak. Tory slammed the now empty glass on the bar, wiped the froth from his bearded lips, and spoke only three words back.

'Cocks tend to.'

The onlookers gasped.

Faith gulped with dread, throwing a nervous glance at Bonnie.

Logan knocked back his shot and his once jovial bullying demeanour took a turn for the worse and elevated to the warrior in which he was.

'Scuse me?'

Tory simply left change on the bar, and with a grateful nod to Bonnie, he headed to the staff area, pushing open the fire exit and heading out into the narrow side alleyway. The Devil wasn't having any of it; he followed Tory around the bar and towards the fire exit even though it was out of bounds for customers.

'Logan, baby, pleas—' pleaded Faith, falling on deaf ears.

'Excuse me, but you're not allowed back here,' said Bonnie. But before she had the chance to try blocking the way, Logan had stepped beyond and out into the darkness. Faith, Stewie, and Robert followed. The small pocket of nosey customers made their way round the bar in hope to get a glimpse at the developing action, but Bonnie laid down the law and stopped them whilst standing at the open fire exit to make sure things didn't get out of hand.

Logan stormed after Tory with his monster-fists clenched. 'Hey...hey! I'll box you now.' The mighty Goliath, Logan, spun David-esque Tory around and butted-heads with him like fighting stags ready to rumble. 'One on one. Bare-knuckle.'

Tory cast his thousand-yard stare up at Logan and thought, *Think I'm scared of your ugly mug?* But, 'I'm retired,' was the only thing that left Tory's mouth.

Faith hid behind her hands at the doorway, knowing this could get ugly very quickly. Tory stared past Logan and into her gorgeous, frightened eyes. Logan gently slapped Tory's face over and over. 'Keep your eyes off her.'

Faith dashed out and got between Logan and Tory. 'Come on, baby, let's go, eh?'

'Stay out of this!' shouted Logan, taking his murderous eyes off Tory for a split second whilst shoving Faith away with his monstrous hand. His mighty strength sent little Faith flying backwards into a muddy puddle.

In a blink of an eye, Tory flared, throwing the perfect left uppercut square on Logan's jaw causing his knees to wobble, then buckle, and finally fall like a house of cards into his own puddle.

Stewie gasped at Robert in shear disbelief.

Bonnie yelled and ran to Faith's aid whilst tragic, gut-churning flashbacks returned to Tory's messed up mind.

'Sorry,' was all he uttered as he grabbed his head in distress.

Logan gathered his composure and rose out of the puddle like a phoenix rising out of the flames and with a killer look, he clenched an iron fist. Tory, knew a punch was coming, and instead of trying to block it, or run away, he simply surrendered his arms out wide, wanting to receive the beating of his life. And so, The Devil capitulated, burying that iron fist right into Tory's face. Down went The Saviour for the first time ever.

Lights out—n-night!

Tory landed hard on the pavement, out cold. A giant gash under his left eye was gushing blood.

Faith and Bonnie shrieked at the violence as Logan simply staggered away into the night, nodding at Faith to follow him. Stewie and Robert hurried to Tory's aid, kneeling and trying to bring him round.

In silence, Logan staggered out of the back alley. He headed for the quayside with Faith trying to keep up with his pace. As they passed docked boats, he slyly rubbed his jaw every so often. No way was he going to show any signs of weakness in front of his woman.

'Are you sure you're okay, babe?' asked Faith, rubbing his giant muscular back. She was trying not to show any signs of pain caused by her so-called lover when he had knocked her into the puddle.

Logan shrugged her hand away. He spoke through a swollen mouth that Tory's chilling threat left. 'You ask me that again, and I'll knock *you* out.'

Flinching at Logan's outburst, Faith simply receded back into her shell and nodded. She paused to put some space between them. Cold and hurting in more than one way, she watched as her so-called lover trudged on ahead of her, leaving her to follow behind him.

Meanwhile, Stewie and Robert knelt beside Tory in a puddle of his blood. They slapped his face gently whilst Bonnie saw to getting rid of the customers and locking up the place for the night; enough was enough for everyone. Tory stirred and groaned as he came to.

'Tory? It's okay—it's okay, we got ya—we got ya,' Stewie comforted Tory. But the moment Tory became aware of his whereabouts, he struggled to get up.

'Stay down—stay down!' added Robert. 'The medics are on their way.'

'No!' mumbled Tory, clambering to his wobbly feet as the distant sound of sirens penetrated the frosty night. Before the two chefs had the chance to convince Tory to stay and be checked out, he had struggled to stand and started to stagger away along the alleyway and into the cloak darkness.

Having stopped off at his local off license to grab a bottle of his ye' ol' faithful—brandy—Tory, still covered in blood, finally made it to the refuge of the countryside. Now on autopilot, he meandered through the familiar yet unlit narrow country roads. The full moon was his only companion.

Shakily, Tory reached into the pockets of his black combat trousers. He lit the last of his pre-rolled cigarettes that he carried in a battered tin. Between drags, he guzzled stiff shots of brandy straight from the bottle.

Now that he had calmed down a little, thoughts about what had just happened rushed in. He couldn't believe what had just occurred. Or how fast it happened. Nor could he believe Faith was now with The Devil. What was she thinking? How did they get together? One thing he was sure of, though, was that he never had stopped loving this fragile English rose and nor would he ever allow someone to lay a finger on her.

As he continued along in the darkness, the consequences for his actions started to haunt his mind. What was he thinking? Why did he have to react? He'd retired from fighting years ago and promised to never lay a finger on another single soul. Now, if word got around of him fighting The Devil, he'd just have *people* resurfacing all in his life again. People he had steered so clear of since his retirement when he'd made a promise to himself never to do what he had loved doing so much…what he was born to do: box.

'Fool,' was the only word he muttered to himself.

Before long, Tory stopped in front of a large wooden gate leading into a cosy thatched country home. Here he stood, slowly swigging the last of the brandy like a man with nothing left to live for. Planted, he yearned up at a tiny lit window. His hand exerciser took the brunt of his frustrations as the light went out. Sighing in self-pity, Tory continued moseying on silently through the night.

He soon approached a milk farm. Vast, dark fields surrounded the ramshackle of a farmhouse. With a muffled protest, the buckled steel gate opened at Tory's push, and he crunched his way up the dark path to the front door. Inside, loud snoring could be heard from the living room nearby. He halted with the squeaky hand exerciser and crept up the creaky stairs to the second floor as quietly as his drunken legs could.

He stumbled into his bedroom. Punch holes covered his door. Cobwebs draped over the dusty broken boxing trophies as uninvited memories of his prime gate-crashed his mind. Tory glanced away in shame. He double-glanced at his already shattered mirror reflecting multiple images of blood crusting his face. His fiery eyes refrained from any eye contact with himself, while a shaky hand, knuckles concealed by his cuffs kept into place due to his thumbs inserted into pre-cut holes, raised a stapler to his deep, bloody gash and he begun stapling it up.

The decrepitly eerie old gothic monstrosity of a house, belonging to Faith's mum, hulked in the moonlight as Faith and Logan crept up the driveway and quietly slipped in. The gothic darkness continued into Faith's bedroom, where the flicker of freshly lit candles illuminated dozens of porcelain antique dolls cramming shelves on the walls. White linens draped over a four-post bed, on which Logan lounged in his muddy trainers. Faith peered into a child's crib and a look of pride filled her face. She caressed her rosy-cheeked two-year old daughter, Alana, as she lay sprawled out, sleeping peacefully.

'Mum must've really tired her out,' whispered Faith to Logan who paid no interest whatsoever with his eyes glued to his smartphone screen and an icepack pressed against his jaw. 'Any news of it yet?' she continued in vain to no response. 'See? I told you. Word won't get out, so there's nothing to be worried about.'

'Worried? I fear no man. I'm the champ! Keep—keep your ugly mug out of this.'

'Logan, cheer up, please? I've been looking forward to this visit for ages.'

Logan prised his eyes away from his phone's screen and pointed to his swollen jaw. 'Cheer up? Cheer up?'

'It's not the end of the world.'

'It isn't? My whole rep's on the line innit?'

'It could be worse,' uttered Faith.

'How?' shouted Logan, causing Alana to stir, sniffle, groan and cry. Faith sighed at Logan for waking her little angel but knew to keep her mouth shut. 'Here's me having to be around whilst you playin' happy families!'

'I didn't make you come,' whispered Faith, lifting Alana out of the crib.

'Think I'd leave you down here for a fortnight—alone?'

'You know you can trust me.'

'Really? Never trust a model!'

'You know I don't model anymore; I'm a full-time mother,' said Faith, hushing crying Alana to settle. Moments later, the sound of Kathy, Faith's mum, was heard as she hurried across the dodgy floorboards spanning across the stair's landing from her room to Faith's.

'It's okay, mum, I'm on it, we're home now, but thanks.'

Kathy knocked and poked her attractive face around the door, 'Okay. Good evening you two?' Faith nodded over and over in desperate attempt to look riveted and enthusiastic.

'Bumped into old friends, didn't we, honey?' said Logan to Faith with a fixed fake grin.

'Oh, I'm glad you had fun, both of you,' whispered Kathy before closing the door on the two.

Later that night, Logan's profuse snoring caused Alana to not settle at all. Faith carried her sweet little angel down the creaky stairs where she could lay on the sofa in darkness in a desperate hope to get some sleep, but each and every snore from Logan vibrated through the house like a petrol mower had been let loose upstairs. Because she couldn't sleep, Faith cast her mind back at the night's events; she couldn't believe she had just seen Tory, after all these years. He looked like shit, unrecognisable in fact, and although she was no longer his, she still cared and was concerned for his welfare. She cared as much as she did when she witnessed this man fall slain, this very night two years ago, in London's O2 Arena.

# Foreclosure

The clock beside him read 03:39. Tory slept soundly, fully dressed and flat on his back with his near-empty brandy bottle still in hand. A magazine strewn beside him. Totally intoxicated and deeply dreaming, he slept unawares of the conflicts swirling about him.

This dream was the dream that he always dreamt. — he and Faith, in a dream world, together, as one…in love. The dream was always seen from the perspective of his very own eyes. Together they rejoiced and played, like children, high on love. They were always in a secret garden with ivy enveloping white pillars and blossoming blood-red roses from ancient roman vases. Faith, draped in a white wedding dress and laughing lustfully, pirouetting round and round clasped in the firm embrace of Tory's safe hands as the twinkling, divine sound of an ethereal classical melody plays. God, did she look divine and angelic… impeccable. Tory never

17

wanted to let her go. In fact, he promised her that, but as the two love birds pirouetted more and more, so did the sudden ringing in his head. And, once again, Tory found himself being torn from his dream from that infernal ringing. With a quick goodbye kiss to her blood-red lips, Tory had indeed crash-landed back down to earth, and, once awoken back with reality's thud, he wished that he never heard the ringing sound of his bedside alarm.

His eyes flung open as his still concealed fist slammed down hard onto the clock, cancelling out the dreaded sound. Tory lay, looking up to the heavens, wishing he was still in dreamland. There he could live out his illusive days with the apple of his eye and escape the bondages he was now subjected to. With a long defiant sigh, he threw back the covers and dangled his legs over the bed.

Sitting dazed and confused, the pain from his stapled-up cheek caused memories from the night before to return to mind: seeing Faith after all these years; fighting The Devil; and being knocked out by him just to name only a few. His attention was drawn to the magazine at his side; the front cover boasted Faith modelling, posing with an older iPhone model from a few years ago just after they had split, in a cover-spread gadget magazine. She looked absolutely stunning and happy no longer with Tory.

'Get a life, Tory,' he whispered to himself and, noticing the remains of brandy in the bottle, he devoured its contents as if water. Tory rolled out of bed ready to face his second job, a gruelling shift down on this very milk farm.

Same shit, different day…

The brown and reds of decay that is autumn falling painted the vast horizon backing onto the milk farm. Calves huddled in a pen as Tory crept stealthily to the closest one before pouncing on it and bringing it down onto the muddy ground. The calf kicked and moaned whilst Tory stroked her snout. 'It's okay, girl, I gotcha—I gotcha,' he whispered, easing her nerves whilst tagging her ear with the gun. 'There you go, there you go.' He released the calf to see her wobbly Bambi legs return happily.

'Pity they're gonna be slammed between baps soon, aye?' shouted an elderly warm voice Tory's way. Tory rose off the muddy floor and cast his soft eyes across the way to see Pat, the farmer, making his jolly way to the son he never had, Tory.

Tory smiled brokenly back at what could only be described as Santa in a green wax coat and Wellington boots making his way to him, and so played along. 'Pat, I think you have your milk farm confused with the abattoir across the way in your old age,' shouted Tory against the cold wind.

The two embraced and shared a flask of coffee. Pat would always bring out his hipflask from the inner pocket of his wax coat and pour a tipple of his home brewed rum into each cup, followed by the same words. 'Here, this will warm your cockles.'

'Hope I didn't wake you last night.'

'Not at all.! Y'know what I'm like after my home brewed tipple,' grinned Pat through his rosy red cheeks whilst pointing at Tory's stapled gash with his hipflask. 'So, who's the lucky guy?'

'Everyone wants a piece of you when they know who you are,' said Tory, lowering his gaze in shame. 'Were'.

'And you let him?'

'What makes you think—'

Pat interrupted in his typical southern country farmer's accent, poking his walking stick hard at Tory's heart region, 'Cos you was the best, you was. You best learn what happened wasn't your fault, and sooner the better, I say, and move on. You don't deserve this self-hate and pain, and you're not getting any younger—none of us are. This will all be over sooner than you think, this thing called life.

'I'll drink to that,' uttered Tory as the sudden, heavy crunching sound of gravel, up the hill by the farmhouse, disturbed the peace and tranquillity of this fresh autumn morning. Pat and Tory cast their eyes towards the low blinding sun, spotting a suited and booted man dragging a signpost out of his sleek company car. Before Tory had time to ask Pat who this unexpected guest could be, Pat had shimmied off the hay bale with a face of thunder and hobbled to the suited interloper.

'Hey...hey! Get off my land! Go on, off with you!' shouted Pat whilst waving his walking stick angrily at him.

Tory crinkled a brow in confusion, relit his rollup and headed up the way to investigate what all the fuss was about. At a closer glance, Tory noticed the man hammering a 'Foreclosure' sign into the muddy ground.

'You can't do this!' exclaimed Pat, attacking the sign with his stick.

'Pat? What's going on?' asked Tory, 'Foreclosure, why?'

'I remortgaged the property last year, and y'know that business has been slow. It's almost impossible to keep up with the competition from corporations these days, and what with the recent blue tongue outbreak...'

'How much do we need?' Pat lowered his gaze, the amount was too insurmountable to even fathom. 'Pat, speak to me!' Tory looked to the estate agent for an answer. 'How much?' but the agent simply blew a bubble-gum bubble and popped it before breaking out the slightest of shrugs. Tory flared up, spitting venom at the dispassionate man, 'At least look like you give you a damn, you heartless smarmy piece of shit!'

'Easy now, Tory, easy,' said Pat, passing Tory his hipflask in attempt to tame the beast—which worked! Tory knocked back the potent shot before relighting his rollup.

'Yeah, don't shoot the messenger,' exclaimed the agent.

Tory didn't need words to tell the estate agent to shut up as one of his simple but effective glares did the trick. 'Pat, how much?' asked Tory again with more conviction, resting a gentle hand on the poor old man's shoulder. Pat sighed, pinched the bridge of his nose and closed his eyes in deep thought.

'I don't know—repayments, plus bills—around two-hundred.'

'Grand?' interrupted Tory, 'Why didn't you tell me this?'

'Oh, it's not your problem,' replied Pat over the hammering of the sign one last time from the estate agent followed by a self-satisfied nod.

Tory felt his blood boil. 'You done?' the estate agent simply nodded over and over at Tory. 'Then get outta my face, before I break it.' The estate agent hurried into his company car and reversed away whilst Tory comforted Pat, who was by now all sniffling and shaking.

'How long we got?'

'New Year's Day. It's over, Tory. I'm sorry. You best start looking for a new place to stay and job. I best start looking for a retirement home.'

'I'm not having you in some home, Pat. *This* is your home, your life, your everything. My everything. We can sort it out. I'll— I'll get more hours in the kitchen or something. We can sort it out, okay?' Pat simply nodded, knowing deep down inside that there was no hope, no saviour, as a single tear trickled and meandered its way through the poor man's white beard.

Tory embraced Pat tight. 'You've always been there for me, Pat. You took me in all those years back when da kicked me out. We'll get through this—I promise.'

'Thank you, Tory. You're like the son I never had.'

Tory watched Pat guzzle from his hipflask and hobble away now as a broken man and wished so much that there was something he could do to help….

# Viral

*The Devil's Gym.*
*Bethnal Green, London.*

Dozens of dedicated fighters pumped weights, sparred aggressively, and shadowboxed amid the air conditioned, sleek, high-tech gym. Wall-mounted flat screen televisions spanned all four walls broadcasting Sky Sports and Boxnation. Buck and Larry watched on ringside as two fighters sparred in the ring. 'Punch and move, punch and move!' shouted Buck through the ropes, 'that's better—that's better!'

Another fighter skipping on the spot watched Sky Sports up at one of the many televisions as the stunning female news anchor moved onto the next story:

Now, breaking news from the world of boxing coming in. Salvatore 'The Saviour' De Luca; remember him? Well, we have remarkable footage of what can only be described as what appears to be ex middleweight champion Tory having a street-fight brawl with the recently crowned heavyweight champion, Logan 'The Devil' Devlin…'

The fighter halted skipping and shouted over his shoulder to Buck. 'Hey, Coach! Coach! Logan's had a fight with the retired Tory!' Buck and Larry swung around in an instance as the fighter nodded up at the television just as the anchor continued:

'…and what can only be seen as Logan nearly being KO'd for the very first time…'

Buck blew his whistle at the two sparring fighters in the ring to indicate time. The two fighters tapped gloves and joined in on the action up on the screen as the CCTV footage played out on the screen.

'Quiet, everyone, quiet!' turn the TV up! Turn it up—up!' ordered Buck to Larry.

As all eyes pinned up on the many TVs and watched on as the footage showed Tory surrendering his hands out wide not wanting to fight as the anchor continued:

'Witnesses stated Logan appeared to be pushing a 'reluctant' Tory to fight.'

The footage played on:

Logan shoved Faith into the puddle.

Tory flared up, uppercutting Logan right on the sweet spot—the jaw.

Logan's legs wobbled before buckling in onto his knees where he remained deliriously.

The entire gym gasped with shock at the footage. The Devil on his knees for the first time right before their very eyes. Then seeing Tory instantly growing submissive, shrinking to the horrid flashbacks playing out in his guilty mind.

The two fighters in the ring awed, 'He dropped him…' muttered one.

'…in one punch,' said the other.

The gym watched on to see Logan rise from the ashes, tower over Tory and bury an iron fist into Tory's face knocking him clean out with torrents of blood pouring from the deep gash under the left eye. The entire gym recoiled and grimaced in reaction to such a hefty blow.

'Ouch!' uttered Larry without taking his eyes off the screen.

The entire gym remained in shock and awe with what they had just witnessed as the final footage of Logan staggering away with Faith at his side leaving Tory out cold with Stewie, Rob and Bonnie hurrying to Tory's aid.

Buck hushed everyone as the anchor finished her story:

'Although worlds apart in weight, the question still remains; who would really win in the ring..? See the full footage and story online at sky sports dot-com.'

Buck roared with rage, booting the water bucket over and throwing his whistle across the gym. 'Goddamn it! Somebody, give me a Goddamn phone!' Larry reached into his pocket and passed Buck his phone, 'And a mop!'

*****

That night, in Faith's mum's rickety old home, Kathy waited eagerly by a closed door for Alana, 'I'm ready!' The door swung open, and out rushed Alana into Kathy's warm embrace dressed adorably as a skeleton.

'Here's your scary lil' Halloween skeleton!' declared Faith proudly.

Logan glared over his phone and rolled his eyes at the happy families playing out before him before fixating back on his phone screen.

'I am so glad you've come down to visit. You know, London isn't really that far away these days.'

'Oh mum, you know it's hard, what with Logan's training n' all. It's a full-time commitment…a marriage.

'Then what about for Christmas? It's just around the corner, and I'm all alone.'

Logan peered over his phone and slyly shook his head at Faith.

'Oh, mum, we'll see. We are here for Halloween and Guy Fawkes, aren't we?'

Logan's phone made a sound; he investigated, and after a moment, he sunk his head into his giant hands and groaned at the incoming news of the fight coming through on his Sky News app and Twitter feed. 'Uh-oh. Shit!'

'Language!' bit Kathy at Logan whilst nodding down at Alana's presence, but Logan didn't give a damn and frowned back at Kathy, wanting to give her verbal abuse but decided to hold his tongue.

'You okay, baby?' asked Faith

'What do you think? It's out; the news.'

Kathy raised a brow at Logan's foul attitude, '*What* news?'

The ringing of Logan's phone soon followed. He leapt up off his seat so fast the chair went flying across the room, causing Alana to jolt in fright and squeeze hold of granny tightly.

'It's okay, baby, no need to be frightened,' whispered Kathy to her distressed granddaughter over Logan's deep, aggressive voice taking the call.

'Coach…playin' at what? Fight? Viral? I didn't push her—she fell. Buck, he gave the lip…only because he cheap-shotted me—I took my eye off him. Back? Now? But I've only just got here— okay—okay!'

Faith and Kathy listened on as Buck's despondent rage filled the entire room. 'Now!'

Logan hung up and paced the kitchen up and down, 'We gotta' go back.'

Kathy hugged Alana tightly whilst looking at Faith in despair, 'What? No, come on, no way. This is ridiculous!'

Faith, feeling she's somewhat on the spot, took her mother's side, 'But we've only just—'

'I'm in the dog-house!' interrupted Logan. Boxing was his life; what he was born to do, and he wasn't going to let two women get in his way.

Faith pleaded her case with Logan, 'Babe, I can't just leave, I've just arrived. I promised to spend time with mum, Alana, visit granny.'

Kathy backed her daughter up; she didn't really care if Logan was around or not. In fact, she'd prefer it if he was gone as she thought him to be a self-centred, obnoxious monster. 'You go then, Logan, and Faith can catch up with you in a fortnight or so.'

Here Logan stood, on the spot with no chance in forcing Faith to return with him now that Kathy was involved and sticking her nose into business that was not hers. 'Christ, okay—kay!'

Faith noticed Logan's nostrils flaring which always meant he was on the verge of breathing fire like some fierce dragon and, wanting to keep the beast from the door, she intervened, taking his side. 'No, mum, I can't, I drove him here.'

'He's a big boy, Faith,' declared Kathy, 'He can get a train, or a cab.'

Faith stared past Kathy at Logan with her soft eyes to simply see her man glare back at her whilst raising a middle finger at her own mother behind her back.

It wasn't long until there was a taxi waiting outside in the dark. Faith rose up on tiptoes to kiss Logan at the front porch but he simply turned his back and shrugged his bag over his shoulder.

'I'm only going to be here, trust me.'

'Trick or treatin'?'

'Yeah, with mum, Alana and school friends who all have children and partners.'

Logan pointed a finger at her bruised face and lowering his voice so Kathy couldn't hear as he threatened her, 'Good, cos' you won't be so pretty no more, I swear down.' Faith nodded as the cab beeped in frustration causing Logan to flare. 'And I swear to God, if that rag-head beeps one more time I'm gonna knock him!' Logan rubbed his swollen jaw and trudged down the path to the wooden gate, 'hate this town already—too small.'

'Faith closed the door and headed back into the kitchen to see Kathy cutting Alana's dinner into small pieces, 'Well, that was short but sweet.'

Faith reached for the red wine and popped the cork, 'yep!'

'Or should I say sour', said Kathy.

'Oh, mum, would you give him a break?'

'No, I won't. I wish you'd find someone decent, Faith.'

'He is.'

'He's not. He's a self-centred twat. And those gold teeth—yuck!'

'He looks after me—Alana.'

Kathy pointed at faith's bruised face, 'It really looks like it!'

Faith subconsciously rubbed her bruise, pouring wine generously into two large glasses. 'I told you, London's a rough place.'

'You don't deserve him—nor does Alana!'

'Mum! Stay out of this.'

'It's true! He takes no interest in her whatsoever! What kind of man does that?'

'He puts food on the table, clothes on her back, a house in Chelsea to die for. What more could I ask?'

'Love. Kindness. Compassion.' There was a long pause until Kathy came out with it, 'What about Tory, I miss him.'

Faith spilt the wine on hearing Tory's name, 'Mum, don't even go there again, please. Me and Tory are finished, okay?'

'I'm sure he'd take you back.'

'Don't you remember what happened after his fight? He like, completely lost the plot! That Italian fire.'

'And do you blame him? After everything that happened? Poor lad. How is Rocco?

'I don't know.'

'Settle back down here. Time is flying, and I'm not getting to hold my granddaughter enough.'

Faith passed Kathy her glass of wine and sat down beside Alana.

'Oh, mum. Would you stop? I live in London now, so get me living here and me and Tory out of your head.'

'Have—have you at least *told* him—?

'No!'

'But you don't know what I was going to say.'

'Yes, I do, now stop it, okay?'

'He has the right…'

Faith threw Kathy a stern look that said "quit it" in front of Alana. Kathy sighed in motherly disappointment and raised her glass. The two saluted their glasses and wished one another happy Halloween before getting ready for a night trick or treating…

# Trick or Treat

Halloween was set to be a fully booked night in the old Custom House restaurant on Poole Quay. Bonnie was behind the bar serving a small group of customers. The owner sat at the bar drinking a beer whilst watching Sky Sports News up at the TV with anger. Tory moseyed in, hammering away at his hand exerciser, and trudged up to the owner.

'Can I have a word?'

The owner, thinking it was going to be about what happened the other night wanted to get to the bottom of it. 'I'm listening,' was all he said.

'You got any more hours, over the Christmas period and stuff?'

'Is this a joke?'

'Do I look like a comedian?'

'Then who do you think you are? Swanning in here like nothing's happened.'

'Huh?'

'Fighting on my premises.'

Tory wondered how the owner got to know such an event occurred, or more importantly who told him. He glanced at Bonnie who pointed with her eyes up at the TV. Tory peeped up at the screen with confusion as to what a television had to do with anything only to see the top story repeating itself on the hour.

'Don't look at her you piece of shit!' Tory wanted to knock out the owner right here on the spot, but he knew he needed his job more so now than ever and so he bit his lip. The owner turned up the television.

The television displayed the CCTV footage of Tory uppercutting Logan as the news anchor covered the story:

'Now, that's one fight I would like to see in the upcoming Grudge Match Series Tour on Christmas Eve,' blared the television.

Tory pointed up at the television with his hand exerciser, 'He started it. He pushed Faith—'

'He rocked up a three-hundred pound bill when times are hard.'

'He pushed Faith.'

'You can't just go around fighting my customers, no matter the circumstances.'

Tory knew he wasn't going to win this debate and simply surrendered and apologised but it was too late. He was told to leave before the police were called. Tory couldn't believe what he was hearing. He needed this job more than ever now and so he pleaded his case, 'Out? It's Halloween—fully booked. Don't do this to me, not now, *please.*'

'You did this to yourself, you hot head.'

'My wages?'

'Will be spent on a new window pane you broke. I saw it this morning on CCTV. Now get out!'

Bonnie continued serving the punter beers and sympathized over at Tory. He simply surrendered his hands when the television caught his eye:

The news anchor spoke over old footage of Tory in his prime unleashing hell on his opponent against the ropes, 'Exposure on Tory has of course been non-existent since the tragic fight between he and his…

In that very instance, Tory had a vivid flashback of releasing a killer left haymaker into his opponent who looked very similar to himself.

*Was it himself he was seeing himself punching?*

Tory couldn't take anymore; he grabbed his haunted mind and turned away from the television, 'Turn it off! Off! Off!'

'Tory?' asked Bonnie before seeing Tory hyperventilating and dashing out of the building in distress.

Outside, Tory keeled forward, again hammering away at his trusted stress release device—his hand exerciser, 'Oh Jesus, oh God…' it had been a long time since he had seen such footage and now suddenly it had resurfaced for the whole world to see again.

Bonnie hurried out and stopped at Tory's side, 'Tory? Are you okay?' Tory nodded, gasping for air, 'I tried telling him it wasn't your fault, I swear.'

'I know—I know.'

'Well, see you around, I guess?'

Tory stood straight and pulled himself together whilst shaking his head slowly, 'No, Bonnie, you won't be.' Bonnie sighed; she liked Tory so much and tried utilising this last moment to tell him how she felt, 'Well, if you ever fancy a drink sometime?' Tory simply nodded coldly at her and turned his back to walk away, leaving Bonnie to talk only to his back, 'She's a fool, y'know. Your ex? Crazy in fact.'

Tory didn't say a word and simply headed away into the night as a broken man with nothing.

Tory stormed straight to the off license, grabbed a bottle of brandy and spent the evening on a bench drinking and smoking himself into a frenzy. His intense eyes gazed out across the harbour, watching the boats come and go. It wasn't just the fact that he had just been fired which had fired him up so much. Yes, he worked down on the farm for Pat but payment came in the form of a free stay, food, bills, whereas working in the kitchens provided his expenses for everything else, but there was something else, something deeper eating away at him right now and it came in the form of the footage of himself he saw on the television screen. It appeared his past had resurfaced to show its ugly face, a past he tried so much to keep submerged in the darkest depths of his broken soul.

Nearly a bottle of brandy later and shivering to the cold, Tory had enough Dutch courage to once again attempt to put this nail in the coffin, and so he rose and staggered off the quay on drunken legs, passing excited children dressed all spooky beside proud parents and all the way back to the countryside. He slowed at the thatched home he always stopped at and fixated again up at the small window, and with one final deep breath, he opened the gate and crept his way to the small door. The house looked so cosy, what with the warm glow emanating through the frosted glass designed to stop peeping Toms from invading privacy. The occupiers had clearly gone through considerable effort for this Halloween night as glowing scary faces carved into pumpkins rested on the porch walls. Tory hid his brandy bottle behind his back and raised a battered, deformed fist to the door ready to knock, and with a long nervous deep breath, he knocked good and proper so that there was no getting out of this one unless he did a runner.

The very instance he knocked, frantic barking from Levi, the family's black Labrador could be heard from inside. It felt like eternity for Tory standing there waiting for any signs of life other than Levi, and just when he thought no one was in, a shadow loomed at the door causing Tory to regret ever deciding to do such a crazy thing. The door opened and with the occupiers thinking it was trick or treaters at the door, the gap between expectation and result widened like the size of a cracked piece of glass to a tectonic fault line. The door unlocked and as Tory braced himself, he found himself standing face-to-face with his father, Franco De Luca. The very instance Franco laid his fiery eyes on his drunken son with a stapled-up cheek, he went to slam the door on him but Tory was too quick and shoved his foot in the way.

'I want to see him!' demanded Tory in a stern yet broken voice as adrenaline was by now well in full swing.

'Basta! Stop!' shouted Franco back as the two pushed against the door, 'You're—you're in violation of your restraining order!'

'I don't give a—he's my brother!'

'You're dead to him.'

'Then let me hear it from him—why you are doing this to me?' continued Tory with bated breath, 'You're killing me!'

'Off my property, you stinkin' drunk before I call the police...again,' spat Franco through gritted teeth.

Tory's desperate aggressive nature stopped in a single heartbeat when his mother, Marie De Luca, soon wisped timidly behind Franco dressed in her usual pinny. His eyes widened and he softened at the sight of his pale and fragile mother who clearly looked like she had been grieving.

'Mum? Mum—Ma! Please! Let me see him! You're killing me!'

'You did that *yourself*,' replied Franco, speaking for Marie, and with one swift, hard punch to Tory's stapled gash, Franco had slammed the door on Tory. Instantly the gash split back open and blood again began to pour.

Poor Tory stood all alone as raindrops began to fall. He tried to quell his rage but the hollowed pumpkins grinning menacingly at him, knowingly, mocked him. He clenched his fists and one-punched each one, exploding them into an orangey mushy goo before storming off the premises and into the wet night like a mad man possessed! His roaring shout ripped through the darkness causing every nocturnal animal to scram or fly under the cloak of darkness.

What a Halloween he was having and unknowingly to Tory, things were just about to get more intense. In the local village square, happy children dressed frightfully trick or treated with their parents. Tory sulked on a bench alone with his brandy bottle and a soggy roll-up cigarette in one hand and his hand exerciser squeaking away in the other. He was soaked by the rain and didn't know or care whether it was blood or raindrops dripping off his chin and onto his black hoody. As he sat there oblivious of all the fun, joy and laughter going on around him, a voice *did* register and resonate in his messed-up mind. That rogue voice broke into his fractured thoughts and he slowly lifted his solemn face to see, a little distance away, the love of his life—Faith. His heart filled with lead and his stomach turned. His yearning eyes grew wide as two full blood moons watching as Faith, Kathy, and a small pocket of friends joyously guided their frightfully dressed little children through the square. Faith must've felt eyes upon her and she glanced aside to see Tory, soaked to the bone and dripping with blood, on a bench and looking right back at her. Tory's fixation on Faith was soon broken when a sweet little skeleton ran up to Faith, boasting a giant lollypop. This sweet little child under the guise of a skeleton could have been anyone of Faith's friends' children, but Tory felt with a sickly sinking of his heart that this little angel was in fact hers. His heart began to bleed more than his face.

'Wow, lucky you!' said Faith overly enthusiastic down on Alana whilst glancing aside again at Tory and breaking an unnerving smile his way. Alana laid her sweet brown eyes on Tory and, as if tapping in to some strange, leftover spiritual connection between Tory and Faith, she left Faith's side and dashed her little legs excitedly towards Tory. He quickly flicked his cigarette and hid his bottle by his ankles, like some naughty school boy being caught by a teacher.

'Alana! Come back here!' shouted Faith whilst hurrying her way worriedly to the bench. Alana ignored her mother's call, stopping in front of Tory and as if oblivious to Tory's bloody face, and broken demeanour, she revealed the lolly to him on extended arm whilst glowing joyously like the North Star. Tory fell spellbound down at the little angel, wiping the pouring blood with his sleeve.

'Trick or treat?' shouted Alana in a long cute squeal to Tory, snapping him out of his spell.

'Um…' was all that left his startled mouth, and before he figured out a simple one word reply, it was too late and Faith was already at her side.

'Come on, angel, leave the man alone.'

Tory crinkled a brow and raised his bloody face up at Faith. *After everything they had been through.* 'Man?'

'Trick or treat!?' squealed Alana louder and bolder with no signs of fear unlike when with Logan.

'Trick!' blurted out Tory to Alana as blood again continued to pour from his gash.

Alana giggled and sprayed Tory with a tiny water gun, causing Faith to raise a brow with total surprise, 'Wow, I think she likes you. She usually wouldn't say "boo" to a ghost!' Tory fixated on Alana and broke a smile, and seeing this approval from Alana, Faith seemed to loosen up and lower her guard a little. Looking at Tory's bloody face she asked, 'Are you o—?'

'She's beautiful,' was the only words that left Tory's mouth. Faith nodded and beamed a proud smile down on Alana whilst reaching into her bag and holding out a baby wipe for him.

Tory gazed deeply at Alana—what could have been. A single mountaineer of a tear escaped and abseiled down his cheek, disguised as a raindrop. 'Congratulat—' was all that managed to leave his mouth. His heartbreak simply muted his words, causing his voice to crack up and his lower lip to wobble. Faith felt her heart break for this broken, bleeding soul on the bench. She saw the man she once knew and was moved to speak.

'Oh Tory.' Tory shook his head and took the wipe from Faith, wiping his escapee tear and not the pouring blood for which it was intended.

'I'm happy for you, really, I am. She's beautiful.'

'Yeah, yeah, she is. Though, you wouldn't say that if you saw her when she's throwing a hissy fit. Sometimes I swear she's the devil's child!' Faith became aware of what she was saying and back-pedalled awkwardly, 'I mean she is The Devil's child—Logan's, just not *'the'* devil, if you know what I mean—of course not because that devil doesn't exist, does it. Look I gotta go!'

'It really is over now, isn't it?'

'Tory, it has been for, like, nearly three years.'

Tory fixated on Alana. 'Yer, but y'know, always a chance and stuff.'

'I'm sorry.' Tory simply stared into space and nodded, watching Faith in his peripheral heading back to the happy families playing out in front of him.

Kathy had watched the whole thing unfold and was heartbroken seeing such a once vibrant warrior now pale and broken on a bench, looking like a drenched rat and a beaten homeless drunk. She picked up Alana, kissed her rosy cheek and carried her along the cobbled ground. Tory reached for his bottle, unscrewed the lid and took a giant fuck-off swig, not knowing the most remarkable thing was about to be bestowed to him from the Universe:

Facing backwards in Kathy's arms, Alana looked on at Tory, groaned and kicked to be put back down, and as soon as her little feet touched the ground, she ran all the way up to him. Tory was shocked seeing this tiny skeletal figure rushing his way.

Faith sighed in frustration and took a step to go get her daughter when Kathy gently held Faith's arm, nodding over at the developing action. The two watched on as Alana reached into her goody bag and passed Tory her favourite sweet of the night—the giant lollypop! Faith, Kathy and Tory were all stunned. His beaten and battered concealed hand shakily reached out to take the lolly from her small delicate hand.

'Thank you.'

Alana beamed a smile through her gappy teeth before running on back to the waiting pair.

'Erm...wow?' said Faith in total shock and awe to Kathy, 'Okay, what just happened there?'

Kathy simply threw a wink, as if All Knowing and simply replied:

'We are all children of the stars, the Universe, Faith, and such bonds cannot be broken, no matter how much *you* may wish it could.'

'What you trying to say, without getting all weird on me?'

'Whether you like it or not; somehow, somewhere, deep inside her? She knows.'

# Vinnie

Tory picked his sorry ass up and trudged through the village town unaffected by the rain like the dead man that he was. Recently, everything seemed to have risen and surfaced. As if getting over Faith wasn't hard enough, but now having her back in his conscious life as well as his unconscious sleeping hours was eating away at him ever more. Seeing her happy and settled with another man and also having a beautiful child together only seemed to rub salt into the wounds all that more. She'd moved on when he had just remained floating around like a turd that wouldn't flush; left feeling grief stricken and guilty for what he caused in the past.

He stopped beside a closed steel hefty shutter. The tatty unlit neon sign above read: The Stinging Butterfly Boxing Academy, accompanied with an unlit neon logo of a butterfly with a bee's sting in its tail. He rested his forehead against the cold steel and closed his eyes in dismay as once beautiful memories metamorphosed into such trauma and total devastation. These horrific memories of his final fight continued to haunt and taunt his guilt-ridden mind. His face creased up as tears began to trickle down his stricken face and off his dark stubbly chin. *How could it all go so badly wrong?* He thought to himself when, just as always, the devil on his shoulder whispered into his ear:

'*Because of you.*'

Rage began coursing through his veins; his exerciser squeaked ten to the dozen as his spare hand drew his brandy bottle behind his back, and accompanied by a long roar, the bottle was sent smashing into the shutter. Shattered glass exploded and rained down all around him as a fist formed, knuckles concealed as always under his cuff hiding all injuries from previous bouts of rage, and with this iron fist clenched, he pounded it into the shutter. The shutter rattled and wobbled. He tucked his exerciser into his back pocket and now equipped with 'two' lethal hands, he began pounding the living daylights out of the shutter. Left and right combos rattled the metal. A dent formed bigger and deeper…and deeper. Old scabs fell off his knuckles under his cuffs as new cuts formed. The shutter would've thrown in the towel, in fact, if it was alive and fully equipped with feelings. The swift punches began to slow until Tory finally surrendered his back against the shutter before sliding down it onto the cold, wet ground. 'Stop it, *please,*' pleaded Tory, 'just make it go away.'

And as if there was someone or some *thing* listening to his cry for help, the wind began to stir autumn leaves around him. Footsteps arose, muffling from inside.

His eyes widened as he recoiled and scurried away from the shutter with bated breath, looking back like a startled cat. The shutter creeeaaaked as it began to slowly rise off the sodden tarmac. Tory rose to his feet. His despondent stare watched the darkness escape from beyond the shutter followed shortly by the long screeching sound of the shutter jamming only five-foot off the ground. Staring into the darkness of the gym a worn pair of trainers appeared before him. Tory sighed, knowing who it was and what more drama was to come his way any moment.

Vinnie appeared casually ducking under the shutter with a baseball bat hanging coolly from one hand. Clearly once fit and strong but now a rather weathered and somewhat starved man in his fifties stood before Tory with a murderous look on his tired face.

Tory lowered his gaze in shame as Vinnie's cockney accent broke the dreaded silence.

'Well, well, well, looky what the cat dragged in.' Tory stared emotionless as Vinnie scrutinised the diluted blood pouring down his face, 'Bit old for trick or treating, don't ya think? Surprised you didn't run away. You're good at doing runners.' Tory remained planted, unfazed by Vinnie's imposing demeanour as Vinnie casually looked over his shoulder to find the dent in the shutter. 'You owe me a new door.' Tory fixated on Vinnie, breaking out a slight nod, 'Cough up!' Tory reached into his pocket and lobbed his wallet to Vinnie. Vinnie opened the wallet and shuffled through a few notes. 'You makin' a mug of me or what? This won't pay for no God forsaken door! It won't pay for shit!'

Tory pointed an unenthusiastic wriggling finger at the door, 'Still opens.'

'Vinnie poked the bat in Tory's face and bit his lip in brewing anger, 'Still opens?' should beat you senseless,' he continued, nodding to Tory's gash, 'like the last mug, you stitched up piece of shit!' Tory opened his arms out wide welcoming a beating, and simply uttered 'Do it.'

'What? Speak up like a real man.'

'I said, "do it!!"' Vinnie drew back his bat.

Tory closed his eyes in welcomed anticipation.

Vinnie swung the bat at Tory's face in full swing, missing him purposely by a cat's whisker.

But Tory didn't flinch a muscle.

All he felt was the wind from the bat's swing kiss his nose and instead, Vinnie followed through, swinging the bat against the shutter. Tory jumped out of his skin and open his eyes, seeing Vinnie battering the shutter over and over whilst shouting his rage at Tory. 'You ditched me! I remortgaged my house to see you through! Us through! To the top! And this is what you left me?! You ungrateful little shit!' Tory jolted on each explosive blow to the shutter.

'You had sponsors—this gym had sponsors.'

'When you upped sticks and ran like a little sissy-pussy, they pulled out. This place fell apart. I fell apart. My marriage. Kids. You ditched me just as we were close to the top. The big boys' league.'

'You had other fighters.'

'Fighters but not warriors. You were my diamond in the rough, the one fighter that comes around once in a trainer's lifetime—if he's lucky. Who had what it took to go the distance—the very top. You were mine, Tory. The best! And *you* blew it. You lost your only shot of a lifetime...my only shot of a lifetime.

'And why did I hang the gloves, Vinnie? Huh? You forget that?'

'It wasn't your fault, Tory. Get that into your thick Italian skull.' Tory shook his head; he didn't agree, and with one simple little nod to the shutter he told Vinnie he owed him a new shutter before taking a step to walk away.

Vinnie swung his bat into the shutter, this time breaking the thing in two, 'To hell with the door and to you. Get outta' here! Go on! Get away from my stinkin' gym! I don't want to see your ugly mug.'

Tory sighed deeply and moseyed on. 'Yeah, turn your back, you weasel, walk away, scurry back to the piss-rotten infested hole you crawled out from. Don't need you! Don't need no man! You hear? You blew it! "Saviour?" Saviour my ass. You're a nobody, De Luca. You hear? You were right, all this is your fault.' Vinnie ducked under the shutter and disappeared into the darkness before the dreaded creaking of the shutter began to lower.

Inside, Vinnie surrendered his back against the shutter and cast his psychotic teary eyes of rage across the gym. Outside light shone through a skylight and onto a worn boxing ring in the centre of the dusty and stagnant gym as memories of he and Tory training together like father and son returned to mind. Life was so good back then, working their way to the very top, proving all the critics wrong, making money doing what they loved most.

And now look at him; standing here, shivering all alone in the dark with nothing at all, and all because of Tory's demise after what had happened that fateful night all those years ago…

Later that night, in the spare room of the thatched countryside home, only the light emanating from the laptop glowed on Franco's slack face. He slumped on a single bed and stared intently out of the window and up at the full moon as crowd cheers and British commentators rang through the speakers.

'Rocco's up against the ropes. Surely it's over,' said Jim Watt, the Sky Sports commentator. 'A stunning left from the Saviour! Rocco is down!'

Franco's shaky hand clicked the mouse as the footage replayed, continuing to poison his mind. 'Rocco's up against the ropes. Surely, it's over.' Franco knocked back a large shot of whiskey and braced himself. 'A stunning left from the Saviour! Rocco is down!' Franco jolted on the sound of the heavy blow, squeezing the mouse with white strained knuckles. A gentle knock on the bedroom door interrupted Franco's private time as he paused the footage. The door opened and in came Marie, switching on the light, having only Franco's back to speak to.

'Franco, he's asking who was at the door again.'

'Carol singers, I don't know.'

'But it's Halloween.'

'Then trick or treaters, Jehovah Witness, the Avon Lady,' snapped Franco, grabbing his bottle of whiskey and topping up his glass. Marie glanced at the laptop screen to see the paused footage of what she knew too well, 'I thought you agreed to stop poisoning your mind with this.' Franco knocked back the shot of whiskey and rose on wobbly legs as Marie continued on, 'Franco, please, don't you think this has gone on long enough?'

Franco chuckled manically and glared at Marie whilst heading for a quick escape—the door, 'Do you?' Franco was always running away from this conversation. Marie clutched his arm whilst seeking to make eye contact with her husband, but it was no use. He yanked himself free and made for the door.

'Just thinking maybe, we should turn over a new leaf.'

'Leaf?' questioned Franco knowing what she was getting at. Marie fidgeted her apron strings and just blurted it out, 'Maybe it's time we forgave—'

Franco swung around and brandished his nearly empty potent bottle, 'Some sins are unforgivable, Marie!' Marie jumped out of her skin and cowered at her husband, 'Don't you dare ever forget!'

Franco clicked the wireless mouse in his hand and forced Marie's head to face the monitor.

'Stop it!'

'A stunning left from the Saviour! Rocco is down!' shouted Jim Watt through the speakers.

'Franco, no!' wailed Marie, closing her eyes and bracing herself. It was too unbearable for her to watch.

'Oh my, this doesn't look good…this does not look good,' added Barry McGuigan.

Franco released his firm grip around Marie's head and the moment he did, his stricken wife surrendered onto the bed and sobbed into her hands. Franco exited and slammed the door causing Marie to jump in fright.

# The Calling

The next day on the milk farm, it was just a normal day for Tory. A smoky bonfire roared as he fed branches and leaves onto it, and staring into the thick smoke he fell into deep thought about the night before; how he had tried to see his brother but instead received a punch from his father. Seeing Faith and her daughter, Alana came to mind. He pulled out the lollipop she'd given him proving it just wasn't some dream. And Vinnie, too? After all these years? All on the same night? Thoughts of where he was going to live and where he was going to work soon infiltrated his mind, adding more worry to his fire. This farm was the best thing for him and now that was soon to be taken from him and from Pat and this weighed on his mind. As thick white plumes of smoke billowed, a silhouetted figure appeared beyond the smoke.

'Salvatore? De Luca?' shouted the silhouetted figure. Tory crinkled a brow and moseyed through the smoke towards the voice to find the fight promoter, Eddie Hearn all suited and booted and beaming a fake Cheshire cat grin on his smug, rich face at Tory. He sniffed the pungent air of manure around him and rudely retched in front of Tory. 'So, this is where you've been hiding all this time,' he said whilst scanning the countryside, 'Nice place you got around here; Peaceful. Too peaceful, don't you think?' Tory simply stood silently with his pitch fork in hand as Eddie stepped closer, screwing up his moisturised face at the sight of manure on his shiny Gucci shoes, 'Don't you miss the roaring of the crowd instead of the roaring of fire?' asked Eddie with dollar signs in his eyes and resting a soppy hand on Tory's shoulder so he could drag and wipe his shitty shoe on the tall grass.

Tory glanced at Eddie's shimmering blinged-up hand and slowly peeled it off his shoulder like it was shit on a tissue, 'What do you want from me?'

'You got the whole boxing world talking again, Tory. Your fight with Logan's got out. Gone viral.' Tory shrugged, faced the fire and loaded more branches onto it using the three-pitch fork, 'There's mass widespread media attention on this...on you!'

'So?'

'Openweight Grudge match. Fight night. London. Christmas Eve. Teeing up fighters with past rivals. We want you to be the spectacle. You v Logan.'

'Not interested.'

'Think about it. Undefeated middleweight hangs his gloves yet nearly knocks out the new British heavyweight champ in a street brawl and all over a girl. Now that's a grudge match.'

'It wasn't over Faith.'

'That's not what the world thinks.'

'Fuck the world! Here today, gone tomorrow. Look, haven't you got anything better to do than hounding me?'

'No, it's my job, Tory.'

'You're wasting your time.'

'This fight would be huge. The story of redemption. The Saviour back from the dead.'

Tory frowned at the Promoter, 'Saviour? You forget too easy.'

'It wasn't your fault. Five-hundred-grand, win or lose. That's half a mil.'

Tory paused; *half a million?* he thought but before he allowed himself to get too excited by the prospect of all that money, stricken memories of guilt, grief and sorrow overruled such a possibility. 'Nothing will get me in that ring.'

'Y'know, sometimes opportunity only comes knocking once. Do you wanna be milking cows and stacking hay bales all your life? This is your shot.'

'I blew my shot.'

'Your coach said the same thing.' Tory's squeaky hand exerciser instantly halted, leaving only the crackling and popping of the fire. The promoter pointed up the way at the foreclosure sign beside his sleek Porsche, 'Foreclosure, eh? Too bad.'

Tory watched the Promoter walk away avoiding patches of manure dotted all over the place and drifted into deep thought, subconsciously rubbing his beaten fists craving the thought. Staring, unseeingly, across the landscape, something caught his eye. Standing right before him in the vast horizon a white stag was there amidst the undergrowth staring right back at him; an Arthurian symbolism for the Knights of the kingdom to pursue a quest. Tory scrubbed his eyes in disbelief and the stag was gone but lingered in his consciousness.

Later that night, Tory sat in front of his laptop, watching the Sky Sports News CCTV footage of the fight between he and Logan.

Meanwhile, in the Stinging Butterfly gym, flickering candles illuminated a makeshift dwelling in the office. Boxing trophies crammed shelves. A gas propane bottle heated a pan of water on the desk. Vinnie huddled on an office chair with a sleeping bag around him as, he too, watched the same footage from his iPad. Vinnie witnessed Tory surrendering his hands whilst Logan released the haymaker into Tory's face.

Tory hits the wet cobbled ground like a sack of potatoes.

Vinnie stirred his pan and raised a brow at Logan's ferocity, 'Jesus.'

Back in the bedroom, Tory continued to watch the Sky Sports News anchor talk about the opportunity he turned down.

'Apparently, the fight has been offered to Tory but he refused,' said one anchor.

'Of course, he refused, he'd get killed. That's why Vinnie, his coach, refused. He's a has-been,' said the second news anchor.

'A has been? He nearly knocked out the champ for crying out loud!'

'When he wasn't looking. Logan had taken his eye off the ball, simple.'

'You saying it's a fluke?'

'Even if Tory took on the fight he'd be finished in no time; First round! It would be like a tank versus a mini in a joust. There's around eighty-pounds between them!'

'Okay, well, I guess we'll never find out.'

Vinnie sighed, turned off the gas from his tiny cooker and grabbed a spoon, 'Yeah, I guess,' he whispered to himself, looking back at all the once proud trophies he and Tory had won along their joyous journey together.

Tory reached forward and switched off the television, 'Guess so.'

In The Devil's Gym, Logan held an ice pack against his jaw and huddled around a laptop with a very unimpressed Buck and Larry at his side as they, too, watched the footage.

'Street fighting? Pushing young girls over? Doesn't make you look good, does it?' said Buck, 'Read what people are saying!'

Logan bent down low and read off the screen:

'Logan's a bully!'

'Tory saved the day!'

'Tory nearly KO'd The Devil!'

Tory, still the Southpaw one-punch master!

'Tory embarrasses Logan.'

Logan's face burned red with anger and rage as Larry continued to rub salt in the wounds, 'And now people know.'

'*Know* what?'

'Read on.'

Logan sighed and continued to read off the screen:

'Tory reveals The Devil's glass jaw weakness!' Logan slammed a beastly fist onto the table, 'He cheap-shotted me! I looked away!'

Buck continued to put Logan in his place, 'Y'see, that's why the ring is the only way to earn respect, with consent from both men willing to fight toe to toe as warriors.'

'I knocked him out, remember? He's a nobody!'

'A no—? Do you actually remember what happened? He was so loved. He was the best, set to go on and break records!'

'Yeah, *was*. Now I'm the frickin' best and people are putting *me* down? They're just his old fans trolling. Have you read my Twitter? I have millions of followers—die-hard fans supporting me. I'd fight stupid little Mario right now, but oh wait, he's too pussy…'

# Bro

Opportunity knocked as Tory left the local shop with his usual brown bag of liquid lunch, brandy. Franco and Marie drove past with a trailer full of landfill junk. He rolled up a cigarette and, with his heart racing, hurried to the thatched country home where he knew his brother was.

Tory opened the gate to the warm welcome of Levi, the family's black Labrador. He stroked Levi, hoping it would ease his nerves. God, was he nervous. It had been over two years, and with a good swig of his brandy, he headed onto the porch and knocked on the door. No answer. Finding the spare key, still concealed in the same old shoe, he gingerly fit it to the lock and slowly opened the door.

It was the first time he had stepped foot in this house since his father had kicked him out nearly fifteen years before, and yet still, nothing seemed to have changed. He returned the key and locked the door behind him. He'd be ready if he had to make a quick escape out through the back door without leaving a trace of his breaking in. He listened hard for any signs of life. The house remained dead quiet except for the beating sound of his heart, racing and thumping hard against his chest. He was more nervous right here, right now, than in any of his fights as he crept on through the quiet hallway and towards the stairs leading up to the bedrooms. Just as his foot stepped onto the first step, he felt a sudden sense of a presence in the dining room beside him. With one deep breath, he turned to the open door and peered round.

There he was. Rocco De Luca sat helplessly in a wheelchair in the makeshift bedroom surrounded by glass framed butterflies hanging on the walls. Rocco's back was to Tory and only the sound of the ticking clock rung out through this unnerving silence. The moment Tory laid his eyes on his older brother, an overwhelming sea of emotions surfaced; love, joy, and elation for seeing his brother alive, yet sorrow, pity, and guilt for seeing him in such a state, but surely this is just a part of his recovery, right? Then, from out of the blue, the tender yet begrudging voice of Rocco broke the deadly silence, 'You hear that? Each and every God forsaken tick...tock, feels like eternity, yet eighteen months in a coma passed by in a blink of an eye.'

Tory felt thrown back from such an opening dialect between he and his brother – no 'hellos', 'how's you?' just straight in with it, and so it was to be.

'Well, it felt like eternity for me, bro.'

Rocco, still in his zone, clicked his fingers, 'Then whoosh! I woke up and I was back here. I guess the question remains; what is time?'

'Yeah, you're lucky to have woken.'

Rocco turned the wheelchair around and faced Tory, pointing at himself who sat helplessly in the wheelchair, 'Lucky?' Tory jolted, his stricken eyes welled up at the sad sight of his once so strong but now pale, weak, and fragile brother staring back at him with soulless big brown eyes and shaking like a leaf head to toe.

'You died for 5 minutes – in the ring!'

'Ah yes, divine bliss! Now that I do remember.'

'Bliss?'

'It was amazing, bro!' replied Rocco over enthusiastically and almost childlike due to excessive brain damage caused by the lack of oxygen to his brain during this near-death experience.

'Huh?'

'I saw everything from above…looking down; the medics, me receiving CPR, papa leaping through the ropes from mine and his corner…and you.'

Tory closed his eyes in anguish as another rogue tear managed to escape from this tough man and trickle down his stricken creased up face as soul-destroying memories returned to haunt his anguished mind.

'I felt loved…free, then the next thing I know I'm in a hospital bed with doctors all around me…enslaved, confined in this vehicle, which I can't escape. Some stupid chair I'll always be condemned to.'

'Forever?' blubbered Tory in shear distress as what first seemed like a monumental day of elation and celebration soon decayed and withered like some autumn leaf.

'Two strokes, Tory.'

The news cut through Tory like a knife to the throat, as the severity of his brother's condition continued to rise and surface.

'Why did I come back, bro? I was free.'

'Don't talk like that, you're scaring me.'

'It's true. There's nothing to fear, bro. Do not fear death when it comes.'

'What would I do without you?'

'You've always managed.'

'I've always had to, it was always you and him, and nothing I did was ever enough to please him.'

Awkward silence fell upon the brothers as Tory's fire seemed to ignite and flare when talking of Franco. Tory noticed scattered dumbbells on the floor, 'Anyway, still good to see you training.'

'All I want is to be able to lift my bodyweight.'

'Why?'

'Oh…no reason.' replied Rocco, eager to change the subject. 'Anyway, you gonna share your contraband?' Tory raised an eyebrow, 'you reek of fags and booze. Don't worry, I won't tell mum and dad.' Tory slipped out a chuckle, opened up the patio doors leading out to the large overgrown garden and grabbed the handles of Rocco's wheelchair.

'It's okay, I got it—I got it.'

Tory watched on as his brother wheeled himself over the makeshift ramp and onto the concrete patio.

A thick layer of mist carpeted the frozen ground. Rocco inhaled deeply and exhaled a long sigh of relief.

'So, how's Italy?'

'Italy?'

'I heard you were living in Italy, having split up with Faith?'

'Italy? That what he told you?' snarled Tory as once again evidence of that quelled fire resurfaced like lit oil on a millpond. 'I'm no longer with her, but I'm still on the farm, where I've *always* been.'

Rocco pondered for a moment in deep thought, trying to remember, when all of a sudden it struck him, 'Oh, that's not far from here!'

'That's it, bro, just up the way. I've been trying to see you, Rocco.'

'Oh, that's nice,' replied Rocco, more interested in the sudden white butterfly fluttering past them and heading further down the garden.

Rocco followed the butterfly with inquisitive eyes before widening like two full moons, 'White butterfly! My favourite!' cried out the now child-like Rocco.

Rocco pushed the wheels of his chair as fast and as hard as he could all in the name of pursuing this elusive creature. Tory remained planted for a moment as the signs of his dear brother's brain damage became ever more apparent.

'Here little butterfly, come here!' exclaimed Rocco, but before long, the arduous task of pushing his chair through the heavily overgrown garden became too much for him, 'Damn it! Stupid chair!'

Tory hurried down the garden, grabbed the handles of the wheelchair and pushed Rocco deeper into the overgrown garden.

For Rocco, chasing this white butterfly was a serious mission!

'A white butterfly; it's a soul…seeking carnation, remember!' cried Rocco over excitedly like only a child would.

'Yeah, your favourite. Always reminds me of you when I see one.'

'How can something that has to go through so much growth and pain to transform into something so beautiful and elusive still be so timid is beyond me?'

The butterfly fluttered high above a bare oak tree with a rope ladder leading to a decrepit tree house nestling into its large strong branches. Two old swings hung from a lower branch.

Rocco awed and gasped like a child at the spellbinding sight, 'Our secret garden!'

'Yeah, yes, it is, bro.'

'God, haven't been here in a while.'

'Me neither.'

'Remember how much fun we used to have here?'

Tory broke a smile as good memories managed to surface from his guilt, 'No matter how much trouble we used to get in we always had each other's back, eh?'

'Yeah, mum and dad stood no chance.'

Tory's brief moment of happy childhood memories soon dwindled and he was pulled back into the dark depths as the harsh truth resurfaced, 'He should never have allowed us to fight, bro.'

'*We* should've never allowed the fight to go ahead.'

Tory nodded to the wise words from his brother, passing the roll-up cigarette to Rocco and lighting it up for him.

'I should've never have fought you,' added Tory.

'It was never me you was fighting.'

'Huh?'

'It was papa.' Tory was thrown back; he had never thought this before.

'God, you two are so similar. Should've always been you two—father and son training. Together, you both would've gone to the top.'

'I would've without him.'

'I was through with it all, Tory. Done with fighting. It was you; the true Rocky dad always wanted, but he couldn't face that fact. I'm no fighter, Tory. I just wanted to live the simple life, y'know? That's who I am. It was you who was the fighter, it's who you are.'

'Was.'

'You're retired?'

'Of course!'

'You always told me the only time you ever felt alive was in the ring.'

'It was true.'

'Then get out there and do what you were born to do.'

Tory shook his head, fixating on his poor brother.

'You're a good man. The saviour.'

Tory shook his head, pointing to the state of his brother, 'I'm no saviour, bro.'

'Damn right you are. Everybody loved you.'

Tory lowered his gaze in shame. Tears finally overflowed and began pouring down Tory's face and uncontrollable emotions finally spilled out. 'I never intended to fight da through you, brother.'

'Well, I fought you to please papa. Why else was I willing to knock out my younger brother.'

Realisation struck Tory how everything seemed to have encompassed around he and Franco, and that it was poor Rocco who was left stuck in the middle of such a feud.

'Hey, you wanna swing?'

'Na, kinda through with sitting, you know?'

Tory felt stupid for what he'd just said all in the name of changing the subject. He took a step towards his poor brother to hug him but his heavy weight of guild pulled him back. He simply stood and looked on, seeing his brother so gaunt, so lifeless, almost simple all the while trembling uncontrollably. Struggling to maintain composure, Tory broke down in tears and cried out

'What have I done to you?

'It's okay.'

Tory shook his head, closed his eyes and faced the heavens. It was as if Rocco's forgiveness hurt Tory even more, opposed to the feeling of atonement.

'It's not. Brothers are meant to protect one another not cripple them. It was over. I had you against the ropes.'

'Really? I don't remember.'

Tory crinkled a brow, 'You don't remember?'

'Nothing at all. And I've never watched it back since.'

'Nor me.' Tapping his head, 'Though it's in here,' squeaked Tory, now on the brink of breaking like a dam.

'I can't get it out of my mind.'

And just like a weak dam, Tory finally broke. He ran up to his dear brother and threw his arms around him as tightly as he could and uncontrollable waves of emotions finally burst and spilled out.

'I'm sorry, I'm so-so sorry, bro! It kills me every day. I've missed you so much! I tried to visit you in hospital, you know, over the eighteen months? But da wouldn't let me. I managed to sneak in when visiting hours were over. I promise, I wudda sat with you the entire eighteen months if I could, I promise—I promise—I promise!'

'I know, bro, I know.'

'I wish so much it was me in this chair, I do—I do—I do!'

Tears filled Rocco's lost eyes, as he simply flicked the cigarette and patted Tory's arms embraced tightly around his neck, 'Y'know, I think that's enough for me for one day.'

Tory let go of his brother and simply nodded, pushing his brother back up the misty garden and back home. Rocco turned, looking strangely at the swings and a ghostly look of evaluation and determination flickered behind his eyes…as if a decision had been made…a look Tory would come to never forget. Tory wheeled Rocco up the ramp and back into the makeshift dining room bedroom.

'Can I see you again? Can you tell da that you want to see me?'

'Just remember that no matter what happens, I will always be with you.'

Tory crinkled a brow with confusion when the crunching sound of gravel intervened. Tory jumped out of his skin, his heart began to pound as he knew he had to make for a quick escape.

'Thanks, for speaking with me,' whispered Tory whilst heading to the patio doors.

'Tory?' Tory froze and turned around. Rocco broke a smile and lobbed a shiny gold item to him. Tory caught the object and opened his hand to see a golden Rocky boxing glove cufflink resting in his hand.

'It's the real deal! Sent by the man himself. I want you to have it, you are the biggest fan after all.'

'It's not me anymore.'

Tory hurried to Rocco and placed the golden boon back into his brother's shaky hand and hugged him one last time, and as he did, Rocco slipped the glove into Tory's coat pocket without him noticing. Tory hurried out the door when his brother had one last thing to say:

'Tory?' Tory halted in the now dark, wintry night and turned to face his brother, 'Ti amo.'

Tory didn't know many Italian words, except all the bad ones from when he was a naughty child, and having only seconds to spare, he simply nodded back at his brother before disappearing like some shadowy spectre of the night.

Tory hurried along the misted garden, past the bare oak tree and scrammed through the undergrowth on his hands and knees until he was in the open field backing onto the country home. The journey back to the milk farm felt like eternity. What was meant to be a visit of joy and elation at seeing his dear brother finally out of an eighteen-month coma, for which he, himself, was responsible, ended only in more darkness and catastrophe.

Tory's heart felt as heavy as a ship's anchor…a broken ship's anchor. He'd killed his brother for five minutes in the ring, then witnessed him fall into a coma for such a length of time, and now, when finally, he thought all the heartbreak was over, life had landed another haymaker killing Tory off once and for all. The lack of oxygen to Rocco's brain, along with the two strokes Rocco had spoken briefly of, had caused so much damage. The thought of his brother being condemned to a wheelchair, trembling like a washing machine on full spin for the rest of his life ate away at Tory's heart like a pool of hungry piranhas. And what about his personality? It was as if he had reverted somewhat back to a child again.

Protecting his family and his friends was at Tory's core. To be the cause of such tragedy to his own blood was beyond comprehension. He would've sought out and killed anyone who would've done such damage to his brother even if it was in the ring and under consent—that's just who he was—a protector. But, he himself was the offender and he felt more suicidal than ever. He felt dead already.

The remaining brandy in the bottle went down like water, and the driest tobacco in his tin felt as smooth as silk; that's how numb this broken man was. As he clambered over a sty and back onto the tight, narrow country roads, there were premature pockets of fireworks going off in the distance much like the words from his brother seeping and resurfacing and illuminating in his brain. Maybe Rocco was right and it was Franco fighting Tory with Rocco as his fists. Maybe Tory was always fighting Franco, too. And so, there was poor Rocco, always in between, being used as some patsy.

All this swirled around Tory, sweeping him up and overwhelming him. He surrendered against a small post box and wept like a big baby, and as he did, his battered fists clenched and, in a manic rage, he pounded the living daylights out of this cast-iron box. A wild roar wrenched from his core making the firework explosions sound like mere party poppers.

This very night, Rocco sat in silence in his wheelchair listening to the dreaded sound of the clock, agonisingly passing by with each endless and eternal tick. Like he had said to Tory, he couldn't remember the fight, but right here and right now he wanted to go there. He wheeled himself to his laptop, loaded YouTube and found the fight. He felt his heart race as he braced himself for revisiting shaking hands with the Grim Reaper nearly two years ago.

The fight played out before him; Franco in his corner shouting tactics through the ropes and Vinnie in the opposite corner shouting his tactics to Tory. Before long it was clear that Rocco stood no chance against The Saviour. Tory was hungry, in his element, whereas it was clear there was no fight in Rocco. Tory saw his chance, an opening, he pounced on his brother like a lion on a gazelle, releasing a drawn back left fist and pounding it into the right side of his brother's head.

Rocco, watching the footage, jumped out of his skin on impact, sending his heart to race more; his brother was a beast, looking almost possessed…zombified. He was unrecognizable, he was…bloodthirsty. As he watched on, seeing himself against his own corner, caked in blood and taking severe punishment, the sudden gut wrenching sense as to why Franco, his own father, wasn't stopping the fight enveloped him like gnarled thorns entangling him.

Rocco watched on, seeing himself being relentlessly chopped down by his own brother whilst just behind, his father, red faced and almost angry, shouted up at him to get the hell out of the corner. With only one eye to see out of, and with both knees buckling in, it was clear to Rocco that he simply had had enough. Dumbfounded commentators criticised the referee for not stopping the fight and Franco for not throwing in the towel. Even Rocco, with his damaged brain and watching on, could see the fight should've been stopped. He saw himself lower his tight guard and leave the perfect open door opportunity for his brother to finish him once and for all.

Watching on with teary eyes, he saw Tory take the shot, releasing the literal killer blow. Tory propelled himself through the air with his left fist drawn, and with a murderous yet focussed look, enough to scare the Devil himself away he released the blow like an express train sending it straight to the temple of his brother. Rocco watched on from his chair as he saw himself drop to the canvas like a sack of potatoes, knowing the lights were already out before his face followed the rest of his body. He watched himself crashing down as medics scrambled through the ropes to tend to him having a seizure on the canvas with white foam oozing from his agape mouth.

'Oh my, this doesn't look good... this does not look good,' said Jim Watt over all the pandemonium as the crowd gasped, silenced and stood all in the name of getting in on the action.

Rocco witnessed Tory fighting to get at his brother to comfort him. He watched him being torn away by staff and security until Tory finally surrendered against the ropes in absolute floods of tears, helplessly watching on as medics urgently performed CPR followed using a defibrillator. Rocco had seen enough; his shaky hand reached out and paused the footage where he simply sat in silence condemned to that sound of the quiet, yet relentless ticking clock churning in his mind.

With what seemed like hours but was in fact only moments, the door opened and in came Franco, loaded with a four-pack of beers and a hopeful smile on his face that one day everything would be back to normal.

'Son, the game's about to start.' But Rocco remained silent, back turned, absorbing each and every tick and tock, 'Roc—'

Franco froze stiff at the sight of the paused footage.

'Why didn't you throw the towel?'

'Scusa?'

Rocco pivoted his chair around to face Franco, with Marie now at her husband's side. It wasn't only Tory who could throw such a murderous look, as the same look glared from Rocco's face at his father.

'What's going on?' asked Marie, sensing the atmosphere.

'Why didn't you throw it?' continued Rocco.

'Throw what, lovey?' continued Marie, interfering with the developing situation. Franco fixated on Rocco and hushed Marie rudely.

'You wanted Tory put down so bad and you did it through me,' continued Rocco.

'That what you think?' replied Franco, again rudely.

'Why else wouldn't you have thrown it?'

'Thrown what?' started Marie again.

'The damn towel!' shouted Rocco at Marie with flared eyes. Rocco clearly didn't give a shit anymore about anything or anyone as the realization that the harsh reality of the debilitated state in which he'd have to live with forever lay squarely at the feet of his father.

'Don't speak to your mother like that!'

'You're a fine one to talk. Like father, like son, I guess.'

'What's gotten into you, or *who*?' asked Franco, but Rocco wasn't relenting.

'Did you really think I could've got out of that?' asked Rocco, pointing to the paused footage.

'Out of what?'

'The corner! He was killing me!'

'I couldn't bear to see you lose.'

'Really? Or couldn't bear to see *you* lose and he win?'

'Huh?' asked Franco, totally oblivious to what his son was getting at.

'You missed your boat! Your shot as a fighter, and sought it through me.'

'I bring you into this world, raise you as a man, a fighter, spent every hour God sent on you, training you, and this is how you repay me?'

'And what about Tory?'

'What about him?'

'Neglect?'

'How dare you. He was a problem child, expelled, violent. He had to go.'

'It wasn't me versus Tory, it was he versus you! And I'm the crippled victim as a result of all this.' Rocco grabbed the laptop and threw it against the wall, smashing it to pieces, 'Now, get out of my face; both of you.'

Marie sobbed into her hands and hurried away. This poor woman never wanted her boys to fight in the first place, and now she was also a victim to all this grief and trauma.

A brave tear trickled from Franco's stern face, as for the first time a glimmer of sorrow affected this strong man:

'Okay, son.' Franco softly closed the door, and once again, Rocco was left trembling alone in silence with only the sound of the ticking clock yet again to accompany him. He faced the patio doors and gazed out at the silhouette of the oak tree with that cold, ghostly look of certainty in his soulless eyes.

The first thing Tory did when he got back to the farm was look up what 'ti amo' meant in Italian, and having typed it into Google the result shocked him:

'I love you.'

Tears filled Tory's eyes. After everything he had caused to his dearest older brother, Rocco had still loved him. Tory sat back in his chair, put his hands in his deep pockets and gazed up at the heavens wishing he had said it back when all of a sudden, he felt something hard in his pocket. He slowly drew the item out of his pocket and opened his hand to find the golden Rocky boxing glove glimmering there…

# Ti Amo

The next day on the milk farm it was yet again a case of different day, same shit for Tory as he led calves into the crooked wooden pen ready for tagging their ears later. Visiting his brother the day before still ate away at him, making him feel more suicidal than ever. It will never be all right, he thought, closing the pen on the calves. How could it be? His brother will always be a shaking wreck condemned to a wheelchair, along with the lights not quite being on upstairs in his mind. Time was also ticking away for he and his father-figure, Pat, as the two were soon to be evicted from everything they'd both worked so hard to sustain and call home. Drinking his problems away wasn't going to make it go away.

Tory sometimes allowed the thought of stepping back in the ring to fight Logan to enter his mind but he soon overruled any notion of such a thing, no matter how badly he wanted to. Not just because of the money, but because it was in his blood and who he was on the soul level. There wasn't some switch you could just turn off and on inside. How could he feed his soul and box like he loved when he was dead already inside? There was no soul to feed so no point in stepping into the ring.

A white butterfly fluttered his way, interrupting Tory from his misery. With tired eyes, he watched this timid creature approach him and, of course, reminding him ever more of his dear brother. But this butterfly wasn't quite so shy and wouldn't leave him alone, fluttering around him before boldly landing on his shoulder. Tory contemplated the butterfly and a sense of spiritual meaning ebbed through him. Lost in thought he was pulled back to the present by the gut churning sound of a dog in shear distress, howling and franticly barking as the butterfly took flight.

Call it intuition, call it a connection, call it what you like, but Tory knew in a single sudden drop of a heartbeat that this distress was in fact coming from Levi and that something very grave was occurring.

'Bro?' whispered Tory with heightened concern. And as the wind stirred up dead leaves and the rain began to fall from the angry, dark clouds above him, he took flight in a manic dash across the fields towards the cries of distress.

Torrential rain and hailstones battered his face as he leapt over the sty dividing the two fields. Tory bolted to the beckoning cries, not having known an animal could sound so frantic. Tory approached the thatched country home in full sprint to find Levi trembling at the gate, soaked to the bone and going absolutely crazy. Without hesitation, at full sprint, Tory hurdled over the high wooden gate, tripping mid-flight and tumbling flat on his face into a mud puddle. He peeled himself up and, with tunnel vision, followed Levi around the back to where he expected the makeshift dining room—now bedroom patio doors to be open.

Levi rushed towards the overgrown garden whilst barking and howling, whereas Tory headed straight for the open doors, shouting his brother's name. Levi hurried up behind Tory and nipped at his heels before hurrying halfway down the garden, continuing to bark, whine and howl as it soon became apparent that Levi wanted Tory to follow him down the sodden path.

In the overgrown Secret Garden, Tory, gagging for breath and caked head to toe in mud, froze stiff. His anxious eyes widened as he dropped to his knees and paled.

'No…' was the only word uttered from his wobbling lip as hanging there peacefully by a swing was Rocco. The faded plastic swing's seat wrapped firmly around his neck as his wheelchair lay upturned beside the rope ladder leading up to the tree house and large branch hosting the swings and now his dead brother.

Levi hopped up at Rocco to try and get him before running to distraught Tory and nipping at his sleeve to do something. Tory remained on his knees with the howling wind and rain pounding his creased-up face as a beaten hand tore up the ground beneath before squeezing it as tightly as he could as if barbarically squeezing his own heart, causing murky water to ooze out.

'Oh God, please, God no. N-n-n-no! Please—please—please…'

A sudden sense of urgency came over his panic-stricken body as he peeled himself off the ground and hurried up the garden, 'N-n-n-n-no…' was all that left his mouth as his chest began to grow tight restricting his breathing until involuntary short yelps left his body. As he bolted through the dining room and on through into the kitchen, tearing open drawers in search of a knife, what was only frantic moments felt like eternity for Tory, when finally—the knife drawer.

His shaky hands grabbed the sharpest knife before scampering back through the house and back along the garden and back to where his poor brother was hanging.

He ran and skidded along the saturated mud and slammed into the upturned wheelchair. He clambered to his feet and aligned the chair below his brother's mucky feet and climbed onto the wheelchair where he found himself face-to-face with the lifeless expression of his brother's greyish blue face.

Tory blubbered, shrieked, turned his cheek and, peeking through one teary eye, he began hacking away at the rope. It felt an eternity as each strand finally let loose. Finally, Rocco collapsed into Tory's arms; his dead weight causing them both to topple onto the boggy ground. Tory lay on top of his dead brother, gasping for air with Levi whining at his side, sniffing to get at his owner. Tory scurried off his lifeless, peaceful brother, pulled him tightly into his arms and cradled his head mother-like, rocking forward and backwards softly. He stroked his blue, pasty face before roaring grief and despair to the heavens; a roar in which if in a lion's pride would silence all roars across the land.

Tory bowed his forehead against his brother's forehead as this broken ex-warrior burst into a crying, blubbering, wallowing mess as ever more guilt struck this broken man's heart and soul reminding him by a simple whisper that he never got to say those three tender words back to his brother haunted his mind:

'I love you, too—I love you, too! I love you. I love you. I love you—I love you. I'm so sorry. Help me! God, somebody help me, please!'

Tory squeezed his brother extra tight as drool dripped from his shaky lip onto his brother's face:

'I love you, my brother…'

His eyes closed and knowing this was his last chance with his brother, fell into a hypnotic trance, cherishing this final moment. Brown autumn leaves rained down all around him almost pirouetting around him like some ethereal ballet as seconds became minutes.

Even the sound of Franco and Marie's car crunching the

gravel no longer deterred Tory away from this moment with his brother, and knowing his time with him was almost up, he held a long goodbye kiss on his cold forehead as ever more rogue tears escaped down his creased-up cheeks and off his trembling jaw.

Levi leapt up on the sound of the churning gravel and burst into a barking frenzy whilst hurrying up the garden, leaving Tory all alone. With his forehead still against his brother's, all he remembered was jolting, squeezing his eyes shut tighter to the soul-destroying sound of his mother wailing followed by the feeling of a hefty barge, knocking him away, as she dropped to her knees beside the lifeless body of her dead son. Sitting alone in a puddle, Tory knew his time with his brother was up as he watched his father joining Marie's side, kneeling beside his favourite, lifeless son. His father, raising his head slowly and throwing Tory a murderous look, through gritted, seething teeth told Tory how it was:

'He wasn't ready for visitors! You meddled with his mind, corrupted him. Turned him against me. And now look! He's dead! You killed our son. He wasn't ready! He wasn't ready…wasn't ready…' finished Franco in a softer tone, taking his dead son's hand and kissing it.

******

It was only a few days until the funeral—a fast burial. Tory dressed in his black suit, and equipped with a hipflask full of brandy tucked away in his inside pocket, left the milk farm and headed through the rain to the nearby secluded cemetery. He knew that he wouldn't be welcomed but he no longer cared. All he felt was…numb, inside and out.

A handful of family and friends stood amidst Marie, Franco around the coffin in the cemetery as the reverend read his final prayer.

'Our Father, who art in heaven, hallowed be thy name…'

Tory watched the funeral through the trees from afar and mimed along to the Lord's Prayer whilst swigging from his hipflask. As he did, he witnessed his mother drop to her knees in anguish, wailing sounds he had never heard from her, adding another knife wound to the heart; how many could one man take? As he watched on at his father and other family members console her, and knowing he wasn't welcome, he simply turned around and went away. Strangely, the only other place Tory felt close to his brother was the Secret Garden…the tree, and thus knowing his parents weren't around, he turned and made his way there.

Levi, once again, greeted Tory at the gate as horrid flashbacks loomed up in his mind. This time, he shooed Levi back and opened the gate properly before giving petting and holding the fine dog. It was almost as if the two, man and beast, had developed a lasting bond having gone through such an ordeal together. Tory headed around the back with Levi at his heels and turned into the Secret Garden. Levi stopped, barked, and howled. It was as if the poor beast was too frightened to recall such a tragedy and venture back to where it all happened. Maybe the poor fellow thought Tory was now going to do the very same thing. Either way, this stricken animal watched on as Tory paced through the undergrowth.

Tory's heart began to beat fast and heavy as he found himself heading towards the tortured old oak that now bore down on him like some imposing beast. Lurking crows flew out from the lisping tree house, circling and cawing down upon him as he made his way.

Tory stopped at the base of the tree and lowered his gaze filled with guilt and shame. He'd hoped to feel close to Rocco here but felt, instead, only despair.

Waves and waves of memories, young and old, good and bad ruptured through his mind, playing tug of war, as the darkness overshadowed the light.

Tory moved around the trunk to the *other side* where the once bright memories stuck to darker ones—his childhood, being neglected, watching on as he witnessed father happily teaching son the ways of boxing while he was shooed away. Here, Tory would venture all alone and, being concealed by the monstrosity of the trunk, this poor child would punch the thick, scaly bark, bruising, cutting, breaking his virgin knuckles at first.

At a closer glance the tree still appeared to bear evidence of all of Tory's anguish as its bark still showed hallmarks of such anguish; torn, chipped, bare patches with dark bloodstains. Having no feelings or means of fighting back, this tree stood to take everything this young man had without ever telling his secret.

But now, decades on, growing out from this battered area blossomed a new leaf. Its green little stem protruded from this inflicted area, as of course with everything in life, time heals —but not, it seemed, for Tory. He felt the fire ignite from deep inside him as his shattered eyes narrowed and his nostrils flared like a raging bull to such dark memories continuing to infiltrate his messed-up mind.

And finally coming to terms that he would never be seeing his dearest brother again; this tree was again to fall victim to Tory's wroth. He fed his thumbs out of the pre-cut holes on his cuffs and scrutinised his beaten, battered, scarred, and deformed knuckles where previous sessions marked the end of his innocence forever.

Tory slowly lifted his gaze, clenched his left fist and with a look enough to extinguish hell and repel high water, he pummelled it into the tree, squashing this new leaf back against the bark, leaving it to hang by only a thread.

God, it felt good.

A swift right blow followed, whipping the leaf clean off, now returning it back to its usual state all those years ago. Faster, heavier punches pounded the living daylights out of the tree. Tory's face creased up in dismay and heartbreak. Deep thumping sounds sounded on each blow almost as if being hacked down by an axe.

Levi circled the trunk, barking and howling as if sensing such a cathartic moment from this broken, lost soul.

Finally, the pace slowed gently to a halt. Tory turned his back to the tree and slid down the rough trunk until he once again broke out into tears, crying into his palms. Levi whined, crept up to Tory, and licked his neck and ear before placing his head onto his lap and whining.

# Secret Meeting

As night fell and a bitter frost set in, it was now Tory's time to visit his brother's grave. Loaded with a bottle of brandy he crept on through the blanket of knee-high mist carpeting the secluded cemetery with only the blue hue of the moonlight to guide him. It was so quiet; God all so quiet. And only the crunching of dead frozen leaves under him made a sound. Tory slowed before the fresh ground burying his brother and got down on one knee in attempt to read the pristine white headstone.

*'In loving memory of our Rocco 'Rocky' De Luca.'* etched into the headstone along with an etched white butterfly on one side and hanging boxing gloves on the other. Tory slumped onto the crisp, cold ground and placed his shivering back against the headstone. Nothing entered his mind as he drank and smoked there on the grave, wishing it were his. He was numb, as if mentally paralysed.

He just simply stared into space whilst shakily fiddling the golden Rocky glove as glowing embers of his roll-up scorched his fingertips. But again, he felt nothing as he placed a fresh one between his quivering lips, lighting it with the remaining existing embers before falling back into another alcoholic induced hypnotic slumber.

As time passed, Tory became cold. His teeth began to chatter and an uncontrollable shiver rattled through his body as this broken man simply continued to sit by his brother's side—it's all he wanted to do. But he was soon interrupted by the sound of leaves crunching under *someone*, or *something's*, feet. Twigs and branches continued to snap, sounding louder and louder as whatever it was approached him. A scanning torchlight illuminated the shadowy overgrown path just off to the side of him before beaming onto him. Tory remained planted on the ground in deep thought, totally uninterested as to who this sudden intruder was for nobody could get through to this man who was dead inside.

'Tory?' whispered the unmistakable voice of Faith. Well, maybe *one* person could. Now Tory popped out of his bubble of misery and slowly turned his shaky head from the darkness and into the light. Faith scrutinised this shivering, chattering broken wreck and crept closer to him, 'Tory, up. You'll catch your death.' Tory slowly shook his head. His look said 'good!' as he slowly turned his stricken gaze back into the darkness, looking up at the moon—the only other entity as lonely as he.

'It's freezing out here.'

'Is…is it?' gasped and gagged Tory in a shivering frenzy. 'H— how is she? The little one? What's her name again?'

'Alana,' uttered Faith, knowing this wasn't the conversation to be having when Rocco was lying dead six-feet below them.

Tory, still fixated up at the moon, broke a smile, 'Alana, that's it. How is she?'

'She's good. With mum.'

Tory nodded, faced Faith and offered his bottle of brandy to her shakily at arm's length.

'No-no, driving. Just came to pay my respects before we head back to London.'

'Where is he, in the car?'

'Don't be silly, he got summoned back a few weeks ago.'

Tory simply nodded, 'How'd you meet him?'

'Tory, stop it.'

'I just want to know, Faith.'

'Why?'

'Just—just for peace of mind.'

'No, it wasn't when we were together. During a modelling shoot, okay?' finished Faith, laying a single rose against Rocco's headstone before crossing herself.

Tory nodded in appreciation and swigged from his bottle, 'How did it ever come to all this, Faith?'

'I know. I'm sorry for your loss. I can only imagine how it must feel.'

Emotions began to break through his numb barrier as clear signs of grief and distress appeared on his face. He bit his trembling lower lip as tears filled his eyes.

'Sorry? You didn't kill him.'

'Nor did you, Tory.'

'I punched him so hard that I killed him for five-minutes, Faith, putting him in a coma for eighteen months. Two strokes later—a wheelchair—for life! I had him against the ropes, the fight was over.'

Faith whimpered behind her open palms as unburied memories returned to her mind. 'He was never the fighter your dad wanted him to be, Tory. It was you, and Franco never gave a damn. It wasn't in Rocco's blood, Tory.'

Tory knocked back another guilty suicidal gulp of brandy from the bottle. 'Brothers are meant to be in arms, not in harms. I never should've fought him.'

'And he should never have fought you.'

'I killed my brother, Faith.'

Tory sighed long and hard and lay down amidst the bed of mist beside the headstone.

'Tory?'

He ignored, closing his eyes as if readying himself for bed, shimmying around almost to get comfy before closing his eyes and letting out a sigh of content, and here he simply lay. 'Tired...just so...tired. Need to just...sleep.'

'You're acting all crazy again.'

Tory shivered, gasped out a little chuckle and quoted with his fingers, 'Again'. An awkward silence arose when Tory's quivering voice broke the silence again, 'Sorry you had to leave me, Faith.'

'It's okay. All in the past.'

Tory shook his head, those words weren't enough, 'You don't make girls cry. Eats me alive. Reap what you sow. I should've known that...being a farmer n' all. Pah!'

'It's okay, Tory. I forgive you, okay? Now get up!'

'For what? It's over.' Faith lowered her gaze, silenced for a reply, witnessing the man she once loved fall ever more into a drunken slumber. 'No brother, parents, job, *you*. Hey, at least you got Alana out of it all. You—you never would've had such an angel if you stuck with me.'

'Yeah...yeah. She's my everything.'

'Everything happens for a reason.'

'Exactly, Tory.'

As hypothermia began to kick in ever more, it became clear that Tory wasn't thinking straight:

'Is...is this a dream? Cos' I dream of this in my very sleep...every night. But you're draped in white. And we're not here, no. In a garden...a secret garden. Shoosh,' hushed Tory with a drunken shaky finger to his lips, 'Our secret. With white butterflies all around.' Finally, a divine smile beamed from semi-conscious Tory flat out on his back.

'You're scaring me?'

Tory ignored Faith and continued his moment he'd been waiting so long for. 'Sad...I know, but—but I sleep purposely j— just to be with you. Feels—feels so *real*. Then I have to wake...and poof!' Tory raised a trembling arm and mimicked an explosion with his hand before continuing:

'It's...it's like I'm with you half my life. I try to find all the right things I want to say to you...but they come when it's too late. And... and now you're here, for real? I still cannot find the right ones to say.'

'It's okay, there's nothing to say. It's over. I've moved on now.'

Tory's face creased up like a distress child, fighting back the tears. His head shook slowly to the killer words received and blubbered like a big cry baby.

'I love you so much, Faith! Can't we give it another go?'

'Stop it.'

'I know she's not mine, Alana? But I would take her in, care for her as if she was my own. You'd both be my princesses, y'know? That's all I would need. And I'd never hurt you, you know that, don't you?'

Now it was time for Faith to be succumbed to emotions, as memories of Logan abusing her verbally and physically returned to her mind; something Tory never did. She simply lowered her gaze, nodded whilst subconsciously hiding her bruised face with her fringe.

'I'm so sorry for all the hurtful things I said! Sorry...for making you cry.'

'You've already said this, Tory.'

'Shooosh, no—no, let me speak my peace. You haunt my dreams every night...and I can't get it out of my head...*you* out of my head.'

'Tory, *don't.*'

'Okay...okay,' whispered Tory, shivering uncontrollably, letting out another blissful sigh, 'Just so...so...tired.'

Faith stepped in closer and took Tory by the hand.

'You're so cold.'

'Physical pain's nothing.'

Faith tugged Tory's arm in vain attempt to pull him onto his feet, 'You need to get warm—fast!'

'Is that an offer?'

'For a lift home, yeah.'

Faith tugged Tory's arm harder but Tory continued to resist.

'No.'

Faith tugged with all her might to move Tory's dead weight. '*You must!*'

Tory pulled and yanked his arm free, 'No, I'm not leaving him down there all on his own. I can't, I won't!'

'It's over,' whispered Faith, trying to make Tory see that there was nothing he could do.

'N-n-no!' grumbled Tory getting again comfy on his back.

'He's dead, Tory!!' Faith gasped for blurting out such words. It was as if by saying it made it all that more real for her. She welled up, knelt beside him, and hugged him tight.

'He's gone.' Tory broke down and sobbed into her shoulder. 'It's okay, I'm here, I'm here.'

'How did it ever come to this?'

'I know, I know. Shush now, shush. It's okay.'

But Tory shook his head, knowing it never would be and simply cried into her shoulder as three muffled words could just be heard:

'You smell amazing.'

Faith sensed the submission in Tory and so she peeled him from the ground, 'Come on,' she whispered, guiding him into the darkness.

Faith managed to shove Tory into her little Mini and keep him there long enough to start the engine and get going and as she drove along the dark, misty, narrow winding roads she glanced aside to see Tory drifting in and out of his paralytic sleep. At a closer glance, she noticed his self-inflicted scars ruining his once proud tattoo down his forearm reading '*Faith*'. She pitied, wondering what on earth this man had been through since they had split. She thought she had been caught spying when Tory surprisingly spoke out semi-conscious:

'You...you still like those strawberry boot-lace sweets? I—I always think of you when I see 'em in the shop. It's like I see nothing else but those. Honing-in like some missile.' Tory mimicked an explosion with a hand, 'Boom. And let me guess, you still like to dip your fries in your choccy shake; your 'guilty pleasure'.

Tory broke out a smile with his eyes still closed as Faith unwittingly slipped out a giggle amidst an overshadow of happy tears.

'Only when alone.'

'What? Not around him?'

'He won't allow it.'

'Come on.'

'Nope. Seriously.'

'Jee...I wish—I wish...the only trouble I had was what my princess liked to do with her...with her...foo—' Tory's hand loosened and his tiny gold glove fell from his hand and into the foot-well of the car as he dosed off into sleep. Faith slowly faced sleeping Tory, slowly nodding to his true words, realising that maybe Tory had changed over the years.

Faith pulled up outside the milk farm and having finally woken him, helped him out of the car, 'Are you all right getting in?'

Tory swayed on drunken legs, 'Sure thing, Princess.'

Faith noticed the foreclosure sign, 'Foreclosure?'

'Sucks, don't it?'

'Was like my second home.'

'Is my home. Don't suppose you got a spare couple-a' hundred grand on you, eh?'

'What you gonna do, Tory?'

'Keep punching.'

'Straight in and no loitering outside in the freezing cold.'

Tory saluted Faith in his drunken state, 'Affirmative.'

'Goodbye, Tory,' she whispered, making her way round to her car door.

'Thanks, for stopping by, anyways. He'd appreciate it.'

'Moving on doesn't mean you just forget.'

'I'm glad you're moving on, really I am.' A moment of silence passed, and just as Tory looked on at this opportunity passing by, he spoke before it was too late, 'Y'know, if your life ever comes crashing down, and you feel you have no one, y'know, to talk to? Anything, you know where I am.'

'Thanks, but you're a few years late. I yearned to be your number one, Tory, instead of Vinnie and ring. I mean, did you ever lov—'

'—Lay a finger on you?' interrupted Tory before Faith could finish, leaving her, again, to subconsciously hide her bruise with her fringe as traces of Tory's fire inside surfaced. 'Y'now, who the hell does he think he is?' Faith halted in the shadows, half in-half out of the car as fiery Tory continued to get worked up, 'Telling you how to eat. Who's got the right to tell you? Stop you? Push you around and lay a damn finger on you? You always used to be a fighter; it's what I loved you for. You—you used to fight back, Faith.'

Faith simply appeared over the car roof and let Tory have it:

'So, did you, Tory.'

'Faith? You was always my only hope.'

Faith shook her head, wishing she was, 'The ring was always your only hope.' Tory stood planted all alone watching Faith clamber into her car and driving off, and here he stood, watching the rear lights disappear into the mist out of sight before turning around and stumbling back the way they came to the secluded cemetery where he simply lay down beside his brother's grave, shuddering violently before closing his eyes hopefully for the very last time.

The full moon passed across the starry sky as Tory lie amidst the frozen dead leaves with a pale face and blue lips. His heart beat slower and slower and just when he was minutes away from dying beside his brother, arms scooped Tory up off the frozen ground, carrying him away along the overgrown path.

# Fight On

After a few hours journey from Dorset to London, and under the dark blue hue of the morning sky, Faith pulled up onto the drive of her London suburban home and killed the engine just in time to see Logan stomp out of the house all dressed in his sponsored training gear. He stormed up to the car and bashed on the window for Faith to wind it down, causing poor little sleeping Alana to wake from her deep sleep and groan.

'What's taken you so long?' Faith clambered out of the car, hushed Logan and lifted Alana out of her child's seat, 'Don't hush me! No one tells me what to do. Thought you was setting off early hours, you shudda been here hours ago!'

'Mum found more chores for me to do; you know what she's like.'

'Do I?'

'Then the car wouldn't start in this cold. It's been a long night, honey and I'm tired.'

Logan shrugged, he simply didn't care and tore open Faith's passenger door.

'What are you—?' asked Faith before being rudely interrupted.

'You're taking me to the gym, dimwit. I ain't running in this cold.'

'I really need to change Alana—get her in the warmth.'

Logan exhaled long and snarled, revealing his ugly gold teeth in the process, 'Here you go again, Alana, Alana, Al—' Logan halted midsentence and honed in on something gold shining in the foot-well of the passenger side of the car. He reached in and grabbed Tory's golden Rocky glove and inspected it.

Faith felt her heart drop to the deepest depths of her gut as she froze in shear fear.

'What the hell's this?' uttered Logan, throwing his evil glare her way. Faith paled, still planted to the ground. '*Whose* is this? Gold…'

Time to think fast:

'Ah, there it is. A—a present for you which I've been searching high and low for.

'Present? You know I hate Rocky.'

'You—you do?'

'And why you shaking?'

'Baby, I'm cold—tired and need to tend to Alana.'

'Where did you get it?' shouted Logan. Faith hushed Logan, nodding to sleeping Alana in desperate hope it would stop this nightmare playing out. 'Don't hush—what did I tell you about—' Logan grabbed Faith by the hair and here she remained frozen in his grasp.

'Ouch! I found it—I found it!'

'Where?!'

'On the ground—the ground!' squealed Faith in pain as Alana

stirred once again and began crying.

Logan walked Faith by the hair as if some mongrel, along the frozen driveway to the front door.

'Liar! Get in—get in the damn house!'

'Babe, get off! It's slippery out here—I've got Alana!'

'Shut your frickin' mug. Got some explainin' to do.' Logan unlocked the door, kicked it open and dragged Faith inside.

Inside the modern, sleek, high-tech home was pandemonium as Logan kicked the heavy door shut behind them with Faith's hair still in his clutches, causing Alana to sob with more intensity and fear. Logan's spare monster-fist clenched in front of Faith's face, 'Last time, I swear,' and knowing she was going to take a beating, Faith agonisingly squatted as low as her tightened pulled hair would allow and placed Alana safely down onto the tiled floor before revealing all.

'It's Tory's!' she felt her hair being pulled tighter, 'Ouch! I—I stopped by to lay flowers at his brother's grave—ouch! He was there freezing to death. I gave him a lift home. That's all. Please, please. I swear, that's all, ow!'

'Knew it!'

'It was below freezing, he was shivering to death,' squealed Faith in pain.

'Let him!' roared Logan, grabbing his head as fantasies of infidelity rattled his jealous mind. 'You spend the night with him?'

'An hour—tops! Nothing happened, I promise. He needed someone to talk to.

Logan buried his fist through the plaster wall just beside Faith's face. She clammed up in fright, seeing her beloved daughter reaching up to her to be picked back up and in her loving, safe arms.

'Please! Don't lose it.'

'Lose it? Lose it? Everyone's slatin' me, putting me down...pro Tory,' grimaced Logan through gritted teeth, 'even *you.*'

'Not at all. I'm here, aren't I?'

Logan pulled on Faith's hair even tighter, 'Did you screw him? In your car? On the very seat I sit on?'

'Ow, please let go, baby, please, ouch! You're just letting Tory screw with your head.'

'I'm sick of hearin' him! Shudda known not to trust a model!' Logan's iron fist clenched, this time burying it into the side of her head. Instantly her legs gave in, supported only by her hair in Logan's firm grasp before being tossed to the hard floor like some piece of junk.

'Now look what you made me do! Always makin' me out the bad guy.'

Faith stirred deliriously on the ground with Alana in total bits at her side. A high-pitched buzzing noise rung through her head followed by the heavy slam of the door that was Logan leaving the house.

Faith comforted Alana, picked her up and carried her deliriously up the stairs into her room where she lay with her on the large bed until once again she finally drifted into sleep. Faith felt the room spinning. Her head was pounding and swelling more and the moment she retched into her palm, the alarm bells rang in her head. She reached for her phone and hurried out of the bedroom. She dialled 999 and eased herself down the stairs in desperate hope to turn the latch so the paramedics could get inside with ease, but the closer she got to the door, the more she felt the room spinning, and after managing to request to the operator an ambulance, she collapsed to the hard, tiled floor followed by her phone smashing to pieces.

\*\*\*\*\*\*

Later that morning and back down south, Tory stirred, groaned, uttering Faith's name, having, yet again, dreamt of her.

'You certainly needed it,' replied a female's voice. Tory woke to find himself in a hospital bed with a nurse placing a hot water bottle under his sheets, 'Faith? You're lucky to be alive, mister.'

'Lucky?' groaned Tory, believing Lady Luck has never come his way before.

'To be found. You nearly froze to death.'

'Good.'

The nurse raised a brow at Tory as he continued, 'Then why did you intervene?'

'It's our job, lovey.'

'Who found me?' the nurse shrugged, 'Female? Faith?'

'Male, but that's all I know. We contacted your parents. Your father answered. Surprised he's not here yet.'

'Life's full of 'em,' replied a not so surprised Tory looking at his bedside at his belongings, scouring for his gold Rocky glove, 'Where is it?'

'Where's what?'

'The glove—my gold glove.'

'Everything that was in your possession is in the plastic tub.'

Tory grabbed the tub and rummaged through to find only his wallet, lighter, tobacco, hand exerciser.

'Damn it!' yelled Tory, swinging his legs out of bed with a one-track mind to go back to the cemetery.

'And where do you think you're going?'

'Gotta go!'

'Not today, I'm afraid. We need to keep you in under observation.'

'Over my dead body.'

'That's what we're worried about.'

'Don't you worry about me.'

Tory grabbed his black combat trousers and checked the many pockets before placing them on over his hospital gown. Next, he slipped on his black hoody before scampering away.

'Um, Salvatore! Mr De Luca!' shouted the nurse to no avail.

Through howling wind and rain, Tory hurried all the way back to the secluded cemetery where he stopped at his brother's headstone and lowered his gaze in sorrow as waves and waves of grief struck his broken heart. Soaked through to the bone, he kept his eyes pinned to the wet ground looking for the golden glove—the priceless boon bestowed to him by his now dead brother. As time passed, he was soon interrupted by Pat hobbling up to him as fast as he can.

'Oh son, there you are! Been worried sick, I have. Searched high and low for you.'

'Sorry, Pat, I know I should be working double-time, but after....'

'Don't be daft,' interrupted Pat, 'after everything you've been through? Though I bring grave news.'

Tory chuckled manically and nodded to his dead brother buried six-feet under, 'Try me.'

'I've just seen your old flames mother, what's her name?'

'Kathy, why what's up?'

'She was on the way to London City Hospital. It's Faith, Tory. She's in a coma.' Tory's eyes widened as he felt another knife jab in his heart. 'She was found at the bottom of the stairs. She fell, Tory.'

'Impossible. I've just seen her last night—hours ago.'

'I'm sorry.'

Tory pondered for a moment as a sudden hunch came over him causing his face to grow mean. 'This is no fall. He hurt her.'

'Don't be daft, son,' replied Pat being the voice of reason.

'I know it.'

Tory hurried to the farmhouse and called the hospital, 'Then when can I visit her?' said Tory with urgency, 'Boyfriend? No, ex. Only close family? But—okay—okay! I'll do that…hourly!' Tory hung up and paced side to side. He knew Logan had hurt her, he just knew it but he of course couldn't prove it…or so he thought.

Hours later and now under the guise of the early nightfall, Tory had just exited his local village shop, and wanting to be alone, Stewie and Robert spotted Tory and invaded his space. 'I'm sorry for your recent loss,' said Stewie tenderly with real sincerity. Tory nodded gracefully.

'I didn't know you and The Devil had made up,' added Stewie, wanting to change the subject.

'We haven't! Never will!'

'Oh…okay.'

'*Why*, what makes you think we have?'

Stewie interrupted, 'He's thanked you, on Twitter, you know, for giving him the official gold boxing cufflink from the man himself. Why would you give something like that away?'

'Yeah, Rocky rules!' said Robert.

'Twitter?'

'Yeah, there's a photo of him holding it whilst thanking you.'

Tory felt his tongue go dry and his face turn prickly as if a million pins were against his face. His heart raced as anger…rage, fuelled by adrenaline coursed through his body.

'Tory, you okay? You've gone all red.'

'That's why he hit her.'

'Huh?' replied Robert, simply oblivious to what Tory was going on about, and without any goodbyes or thanks, Tory had again vanished into the darkness like a man on a serious mission.

Tory ran along the winding country roads filled with rage crackling like fireworks. He reached the Stinging Butterfly gym as fast as his tired legs could carry him and breathlessly pounded the living daylights out of the shutter. Moments later the shutter slowly rose. Tory paced side to side whilst thrashing away at his hand exerciser as the shutter jammed followed by Vinnie appearing out of the shadows with a psychotic look.

'Don't you know how to knock polite?'

Tory simply glared at Vinnie with angry yet broken eyes.

'I want in. I want to fight that piece of shit.'

'You V The Devil?'

'He hurt her.'

'Sounds like your problem.'

'Hundred grand.'

'I want nothing to do with you.'

'Hundred and fifty.'

'Nope.'

'Vinnie, don't make me go at it alone.'

'You do that. Get life cover,' snarled Vinnie before disappearing into the dark depths of the gym, closing the shutter on Tory. Vinnie rested his shivering back against the shutter in total darkness and pondered the offer; a hundred and fifty grand do what he loved most which would certainly get him out of the shit he was in, but stubbornness and hate for Tory overruled any thought of working alongside him again; he ruined his life after all.

Inside a barn on the milk farm, bales of hay stacked the wooden structure. Inside, Tory paced side-to-side thrashing his exerciser whilst taking a call to the London met hospital. Moon rays beamed through the skylight, cutting through the darkness, onto a hanging leather dusty punch bag. The call soon came to an end; there was still no progress in Faith's current condition as Tory sighed and slumped his sorry ass onto a hay bale and swigged from his brandy bottle. He stared lost into space with teary eyes, retching to the onslaught of brandy his body was consuming. He screwed his face at the sight of the bottle and launched it against the wooden wall, smashing it to pieces. He lowered his head into his hands and sobbed when from out of the shadows came a subtle creaking noise on this still night. Tory crinkled a brow and raised his head from out of his hands to find the hanging bag swaying subtly to and fro from under the pale-blue moonlight. A white butterfly appeared out of the shadows and fluttered around the hanging bag.

Tory's eyes grew wide, watching the butterfly dance around the bag before landing on it.

'Bro?'

Tory rose to his feet, crept to the bag in shear disbelief and stepped out of the shadows and into the moonlight where he stood face to face with the heavy bag. He slowly fed his thumbs out of his cuffs concealing his knuckles revealing, once again, his scabby, scarred, deformed fists. His fingers caressed the dusty, mouldy bag. The butterfly took flight and so leaving Tory to what was to come...

Tory's face grew mean.

A concealed left fist slammed into the bag.

Settled dust took flight and floated around him twinkling like glittering fairy dust as another swift, hard punch appeared out of the shadows and into the bag.

'Bastard...bastard!' roared Tory as faster, harder combination blows hacked into the bag. The white butterfly danced around Tory, circling him as if his brother was with him, supporting him, right here, right now. Tory finished torturing this bag with a hefty left blow, and as he turned to run out into the darkness, he was greeted to the sight of Pat at the barn's entrance surrounded by shattered glass.

'You okay, son?'

Tory stared long and hard at Pat with the bag swinging and creaking behind him and with the decision already made he simply replied, 'Fight on.'

Pat simply nodded and stepped out of the way leaving Tory to break out into a forceful run, disappearing into the darkness like some hero of the night...

# Doing it Alone

Customers sat at a table in the old Custom House and waited anxiously for their food in Bonnie's arms. Bonnie fixated up at the TV screen with full plates in her hand as the sports news anchor discussed the upcoming fight:

'A few days back you might have heard us mention the feud between Logan and Tory, and how Tory turned down the offer to fight Logan. Well, fresh off the press, he's back from the dead and accepted the challenge! Salvatore 'The Saviour' De Luca is fighting Logan 'The Devil' Devlin this Christmas Eve in the upcoming Grudge Match series brought to you by Everlast. Can you believe it?'

'Yes! Yes—yes—yes!' yelled Bonnie to the grand news, disturbing customers indulging in their food all around her. The table of waiting customers beside her cleared their throats purposely up at Bonnie, wanting their plates of food balanced so intricately in her arms. 'Oh, sorry—sorry—sorry!' said Bonnie, serving the plates before hurrying into the kitchen to break the news to Stewie and Robert, 'He's fighting! He's bloody fighting! Christmas Eve!' Stewie and Robert high-fived one another, delighted by the news that their friend was back in action.

04:30am and whilst most of the village was sleeping, Tory, dressed in grey training gear attempted pumping out press-ups, but being out of shape for so long, collapsed flat on his face onto the hard floorboards after only a dozen or so.

Later that morning, and with the hue of the dark blue sky edging brighter as the sun began to rise, stood Tory amidst a scrap heap on the milk farm, dragging out a rusty car axel and using it to pump out bicep curls, but again caved in after only a few reps.

He laid flat on his back and used the axel to bench-press, again, after only a few reps, felt the burn due to being out of shape for so long.

The low winter sun broke out across the naked horizon. Tory stood before a swing-ball post used normally for hitting a tennis ball in counter directions with a friend but not today. Tory grabbed the ball attached to thin rope and hurled it, and as the ball swung round and round, Tory attempted using his fists to send the ball in the counter direction but failed miserably, missing the ball time after time.

As the day grew fresh, Tory grew ever more tired and fatigued. He leapt up onto a low branch and hanged, straining to attempt a pull-up before yelling, letting go and falling flat on his face onto the grass.

However tired he felt, this warrior knew it was no overnight process to get into shape for a fight, and standing at the top of a small rock pile, Tory swung a sledgehammer down onto a boulder. Only tiny pieces of stone propelled into the air as he wiped beads of sweat from his brow before swinging the sledgehammer relentlessly again, and again…and again.

Tory then loaded the piles of rocks into a rusty wheelbarrow and pushed with all his might to get the squeaky buckled wheel moving. The barrow keeled to one side, tipping the pile of rocks all over the sodden ground.

'This fight has gathered momentum and gained real exposure all across the boxing world; the fans included. This event is now set to be a sell-out,' said the sports news anchor as Franco sat in the traditional living room watching the news, drinking himself into a drunken slumber. His shaky hand poured another large quantity of whiskey into a glass as the news anchors discussed and debated the upcoming fight.

'But there's no belt up for grabs,' said one anchor.

'It's an open weight fight which we never get to see, that's what's so exciting about this fight, whether a title fight or not,' replied another.

Franco hurled the TV remote across the room in rage. He was so spiteful that Tory had got back into fighting when causing what he had done to Rocco.

Vinnie huddled in his sleeping bag in the makeshift living quarters of the office, watching the same debate on his iPad.

'He's going at it alone,' continued the news anchor, 'he has no manager. No manager means no gym, no mentor, no support.'

Vinnie sighed deep, fixating on the many trophies on the shelf, wanting to, deep down, take Tory up on the offer training him but stubbornness and blame for Tory ruining his life yet again intervened.

'So far he's been well out of the media and social media; no Facebook, Twitter, nothing. Will we be seeing him tomorrow at the press conference remains the question on everybody's lips…'

That night, Stewie and Robert smoked a cigarette in the alleyway by the fire exit of the old Custom House when Tory jogged up to them.

'Hey man, congratulations on taking on the big fight,' said Stewie proudly.

'You still want some tips?'

'Wet floors can be slippery, yeah I got it,' replied Stewie.

'You wanna train?'

'With you?'

'Yeah.'

'Hell yeah! When I'm not at my designated gym and here, of course.'

Tory agreed; Stewie embraced Tory in gratitude. Tory took the cigarette from Stewie, tossed it down the drain and jogged on.

Stewie faced his brother, star struck to the news, 'You hear that, bro? I'm training with the Saviour!'

\*\*\*\*\*\*

Tory hopped on a train and made his few hours' trip to London ready for the press conference the next day. From Waterloo Station, he took a black cab journey to London City Hospital before heading on to his hotel. He gazed out of the window at all the city lights and hustle and bustle of the Capital as grave thoughts of Faith continued to haunt his mind, just adding to the tragedy of everything's that'd recently happened.

The receptionist inside the hospital pointed the way for Tory. The walk along the corridor felt like eternity as his heart began to race; he was so nervous in anticipation for seeing Faith. Tory opened the door and crept in to see Faith lying peacefully wired up to bleeping machines.

'Princess?' he whispered, sitting quietly at her side. His beaten, battered, killer hands tenderly stroked and held Faith's tiny, delicate hand as his bottom lip wobbled and tears filled his eyes, 'It's me, Tory. The dumbass who let you go. I'm fighting him, so you got nothin' to worry about no more, okay? When you wake, it will be all over. You'll be free. Just hang in there, okay? Stay strong, yeah? Keep punching, my little fighter. You've always been a fighter.'

Tory watched on at the love of his life lying silently before him like Sleeping Beauty. A giant black bruise ruined one side of her face from not only Logan's might punch but the impact of hitting the hard, tiled floor. 'Look at you,' he blubbered, resting his forehead against her, 'I love you, Faith.'

The door opened softly; Tory jumped out of his skin and threw his head around at the door, thinking at first it was The Devil, but in crept Kathy who froze stiff at the site of someone in the shadows next to her daughter. Tory stood up respectively.

'Who's there?' she asked.

'Me…Tory,' he whispered, offering the chair to Kathy.

Kathy hurried up to him and threw her arms around him, sobbing into his shoulder. 'Oh, Tory. My poor baby.'

'I know, I know.'

'She and Alana are all I have.'

'I know, shush now, I know. She okay? Alana?'

'With his parents. I'm getting her later.'

'That's good, that's good.'

'People don't just fall down stairs, Tory.'

'I know.'

'If that bastard dared to lay a finger on my daughter—'

'It's okay, I'm here, I'm here.'

'What do we do, Tory? The police aren't accepting any accusations until they have interviewed her.'

'I'm fighting him. Christmas Eve. He won't be able to lay a brick, let alone a finger when I'm done with him.' Tory controlled his rage, holding the chair out for Kathy to sit. She perched on the edge of the chair and held Faith's hand.

'I feel so helpless.'

'You okay? You need anything?'

'Maybe a coffee or something?'

'Sure, sure thing.'

Tory headed to the door.

'Tory? I've missed you.'

'I've missed you, too.'

That night, the two sat at Faith's side, mostly in silence, until visiting times were over. The closer Tory made his way to the exit door, the more rage and anger he felt surfacing. He stormed out of the automatic door and keeled forward, panting for air as patients and visitors smoking cigarettes looked on at him.

The winds of change stirred dead leaves by his feet.

His fiery, teary eyes closed.

Battered knuckles strained white, and unable to quell this rage any longer, he roared. Veins and muscles popped out of his neck, and as one pissed off Italian, he ran along the path to his hotel room.

# Truth Hurts

Swarms of Press waited eagerly outside the doors of the press conference with cameras at the ready when a black cab slowed beside them. The passenger door kicked open and out Tory leapt like a madman on a mission. He stormed past the Press towards the entrance.

'Tory!' shouted one member of the Press.

'Salvatore!' shouted another, trying to get his attention.

'What finally made you accept the challenge?'

'You don't really think you can beat this slab of meat, do you?'

'Where's your manager?'

'Tory, welcome back. Does this mean you're out of retirement for good?' shouted another, trying to get a word in edgeways but it was no use; Tory barged through the Press and pushed open the entrance door.

Officials led the way to the conference room with Tory following like a raging bull.

Eddie Hearn and more press and officials filled the room. Logan sat on edge in front of the packed room answering questions with Buck and Larry at his side.

'What made me take on the fight?' replied Logan to the member of the press who had asked the question.

'Yeah, being a non-title fight n' all.'

'To prove to y'all that it was a fluke. A cheap shot. That he's a fluke, a has-been.'

'Have the police questioned you yet from that night?' asked another.

'Police? Why?'

'For starting the fight—pushing Faith over. That's quite a serious offence.'

'Offence?' snarled Logan, 'she didn't press charges—she's my girl; I didn't know my own strength. That's it. Next question.'

The double doors burst open, causing the attention to focus on the door. Camera flashes lit up the door. Tory stormed in heading right for Logan with satanic eyes.

'Here's Tory now!' exclaimed the press conference commentator.

'Tripped down the stairs? You bastard, coward!'

Logan jumped to his feet and clenched his iron fists, 'Screwing my girl?' shouted Logan, having to be restrained by Buck and Larry whilst beef-cake security held Tory back from Logan, struggling to contain this psychotic wriggly worm.

'Never touched her! Get off! Let me at him! Get off!' yelled Tory, kicking and screaming to get at The Devil.

'Tory is enraged!' continued the press conference commentator.

Logan revealed the gold glove to Tory, pinching it between finger and thumb, 'Thanks for the pressie.'

Tory's eyes widened, raging and tearing more so to get at The Devil.

Logan smirked down at Tory, winking.

'Give it! My—my brother's!' wailed Tory as waves and waves of emotions poured out of this grief-stricken man.

'Finders keepers, bitch.'

Eddie Hearn stood between Logan on the stage and Tory below, 'Woh— woh! Save it for the ring—the ring!'

A member of the press held out his Dictaphone to Tory, 'Why this sudden grudge?'

'He hit her!' roared Tory still transfixed on Logan, 'He always hit her.'

'Never touched her.'

'She's in a coma! I'm exposing you right now!'

'That's quite some accusation,' added the member of the press as security dragged Tory away.

'Gonna kill him!' continued Tory.

'You're punching above your weight, De Luca! You'll be joining your brother, y'know, the one you retarded?'

Tory flared ever more, roaring, fighting with all his might, love and guilt to free himself and get to Logan.

'Oh, this is really getting out of hand,' added the commentator. Inches from the exit door, Tory pointed the finger with murderous eyes, 'You might be taller than me, you might be bigger than me, you might be stronger than me, but I'm comin' for you, and I'm willing to die tryin'! I'm gonna' knock that golden smug grin off your face! Now it's personal.'

And on that note, the doors closed and an eerie silence fell upon the room leaving only Tory's shouts to be heard muffling through the door.

'This fight has spiralled, snowballed out of control,' said the commentator, 'and has to be the most anticipated fight since Logan's recent fight with Joshua. There's no love-loss here. But one thing is for sure, we're in for one hell of a fight come Christmas Eve.'

Vinnie huddled in his sleeping bag, watching the press conference on his iPad as the words from the commentator played out:

'There's no love-loss here.'

Vinnie paused the footage and broke a smile as signs of respect shone through.

'That's my boy.'

\*\*\*\*\*\*

The next day, Tory, back in his training gear, knelt on one knee in prayer at his brother's grave, 'Just this once, I promise.'

Twigs on the frozen ground snapped behind him. He opened his eyes and dreaded, knowing, for some strange reason that it was his father. He closed his eyes in dismay as his father's stern, unforgiving voice disturbed the peace.

'Back from the dead?'

'What do you care?' replied Tory fixating on the pristine white headstone when suddenly he felt a hand around the back of his neck shoving him against the headstone.

'Think you deserve having your life back? Huh?'

Tory squeezed his eyes shut, not bearing to allow his father's words to brainwash him, and as he remained here poised, the sound of Marie's quick steps approached followed by her wail.

'Franco, please!'

'Think I'm stupido?' continued Franco, ignoring his wife's plea, 'You broke in. Poisoned his mind. Turned him against me.'

'You just can't let it go, can you?'

'He wasn't ready for visitors! He was high-risk, and now look what happened!' shouted Franco, pushing Tory's face hard against the headstone and bending his nose to the brink of breakage if it wasn't for such soft cartilage from previous breakages.

'Franco, let go of him! *Now*!'

Franco let go of Tory, allowing him to slowly turn around and face his parents to let them have it.

'Don't you think I also wish it was me down there instead of him? Your precious son? You know, I realized it really doesn't matter whether I fought him or not, you've never cared. It was always you two. Always. From day one; you and him, father and son trainin', bonding. What about me? How do you think that made me feel, huh? Having to find my role-model someplace else…in someone else. Never watchin' a single fight of mine. I was the best! *Your* Rocky.' Tory sighed deep and softened as his soul's yearning for such a life crumbled before him, 'It couldda' been me n' you. Shudda'. You know what, I think like all bullies you're only blaming others to cover your own guilt.'

'What you talking about?'

'Are you blaming me cos' really you blame yourself?'

'I have nothing to be sorry for.'

'Why didn't you throw the towel?'

Franco grabbed Tory and pressed his face back against the headstone as hard as he could. Tory took the pain.

'I do wish it was you down there. You killed our son.'

Marie broke down and cried into her hands.

Tory, on his knees in pain and yelping for air, shook his head slowly and fought back with words, 'No, da, you did that yourself.'

He closed his eyes expecting a punch to the head as indeed Franco clenched his fist, but Marie slapped Franco's fist and hurried away causing Franco to relent and trudge away.

Tory remained on his knees, ever more broken inside and closed his eyes, overwhelmed for this contact with his father. And as he sighed long and deep upon hearing their footsteps dilute away from him there was still a visitor who wasn't quite done with him yet…

'Y'know, I really don't like that mug,' said the voice.

Tory jumped out of his skin and turned around like a deer in headlights as right there, right before him, was Vinnie standing solemnly with his hands in his coat pockets. Tory sighed, expecting more grief now from his ex-coach.

'Who, The Devil, or him?'

'Both,' uttered Vinnie, looking to the direction of Franco before breaking a smile down on Tory.

Tory smiled back and chuckled.

Vinnie chuckled until they both erupted into laughter but moments later, the sight of his brother's headstone caused Tory to relent, mute and lower his gaze in shame and guilt. 'I understand you had to do what you had to do, Tory, even if it meant hanging the gloves. All I can say is I'm sorry for your loss, really I am.'

'Thank you.'

'Now get up off one knee, we got a fight to train for, besides, people will start talking.'

'We?'

Vinnie offered out his hand to Tory.

Tory fixated on the open hand and grabbed it to be pulled up onto his feet.

'We. Now let's do this, got an electricity bill to pay.' Tory chuckled and limped away with Vinnie reconciled at his side.

That night, Franco kicked open the front door of his countryside home enraged from the harsh true words he had received from his hated estranged son. He stormed into the kitchen, tore open the cupboard housing the whiskey and reached for the bottle.

'I can't believe you just said that to him,' said Marie joining his side with more power and vigour in her voice than ever before.

'Truth hurts,' snapped Franco, pouring whiskey into a large

glass and bringing it to his lips, and just as he expected the warm, potent relief to succumb to him, harsh, true words from Marie finally came his way:

'No, Franco. No.'

Franco halted with the rim of the glass on his lips, 'Scusa?' Marie transfixed on a wall photo of Rocco with a white butterfly resting on his finger and shook her head slowly, 'He did it all for you. It wasn't who he was. He wasn't a fighter. You pushed him to fight. *You*! To fill some void you missed out on. You had a second son the spitting image of you, who had what it took...' Franco lowered the glass from his lips and slowly faced Marie in confusion as she continued to talk to him all the while transfixing on the photo and pointing to the door, '...Tory. Rocco had had enough.' Realization struck her as she broke away from the photo and treaded closer to Franco, 'He...he would still be here now if it wasn't for *you*,' she added, picking up pace with a lost glazed expression on her pale face, 'You killed our son!' She backhanded the glass of whiskey out of her shocked husband's hand and slapped him in the face. Franco took the heavy slaps as her slaps turned to thumps on his chest. You killed my boy! And so, you killed me.' Franco took the frantic beating thumps to his chest, 'And now you've killed my only son left.'

Franco swiped the whiskey bottle off the kitchen worktop, turned his back on Marie and headed silently along the hall, leaving Marie to wail and break down into pieces on the hard, tiled kitchen floor...

# Training

5am the next morning and under the cloak of darkness, the Stinging Butterfly's shutter creaked open and rose. Tory and Stewie hopped on the spot in training gear and ready for action with Vinnie at their side.

'We're cutting this fine, too fine,' said Vinnie to Tory, 'Under eight weeks. We ain't got long enough to train to go the distance. I say we got four rounds, max! Anything beyond that is the danger zone. You're outta shape. Fighting a man in his prime, at the top of his game—double your size. Rage won't win this fight, but only your heart. We gotta lot of time to make up, and weight!' Vinnie set his stopwatch, 'First up, roadwork. With weight!'

Stood before the unforgiving killer hills of Lulworth, along the Dorset Jurassic coast, and loaded with 35lbs of weight in their rucksacks Tory and Stewie broke out into a run on Vinnie's whistle.

'Thought he said roadwork?' asked Stewie, quivering at the size of the infinite sweeping hills ahead.

'Tell me about it,' uttered Tory, knowing the pain to come.

Franco sat on the sofa in the living room watching CNN; an American news channel in desperate hope to stay away from Tory and his plight, but there was no escape as the topic of conversation between the stunning female news anchor and her male counterpart soon changed to Tory's fight:

'Now,' started the female anchor, 'following the Everlast Grudge Match tour which has now travelled across the pond to London: A feud between two unlikely British boxers has spiralled out of control and gathered mass media attention across the entire boxing world.' Franco reached for the TV remote but something inside him stopped him from changing the channel, and so, he watched on reluctantly as the male anchor took over, 'A middleweight fighter, Salvatore 'The Saviour' De Luca, retired after paralysing his brother in the British Championships accepts to fight the new British heavyweight champion, Logan 'The Devil' Devlin in what can only be explained as vengeance for what The Saviour calls 'woman beating'.

'So, let me get this straight,' started the male news anchor, 'the retired middleweight—'

'The Saviour,' interrupted the female anchor.

'Right, the Saviour, once dated the heavyweight's girl and now wants to fight him because he's accusing him of hospitalising her?'

'Precisely that.'

'Well, if that's not true love then I don't know what is. They'll be all eyes on this openweight fight live on Box Office come Christmas Eve.' Franco switched off the TV feeling some kind of respect for his son fighting for the love of his life.

4am the next morning and feeling rather tender from the epic run the day before, Tory stood before his shattered mirror and necked a pint of half-a-dozen eggs before pulling his hoody over his head and hurrying out of his room, down the wooden stairs and out of the front door. He jogged onto the icy path and leapt over the steel gate and continued onto the narrow country roads without seeing a member of the paparazzi taking snaps from behind a rusty tractor.

Later that morning in London, Logan slept soundly in his nice warm comfy bed, snug as a bug in a rug whilst Tory pounded the living shit out of the heavy hanging bag in the dark gym, having only the natural outside light to come through the skylight and open shutter. Stewie skipped on the spot with a skipping rope.

'One more minute then swap!'

As the days grew on, the more Tory and Stewie's training intensified:

Tory pounded Stewie's padded mitts, 'Faster—faster! One—two duck, one—two duck! That's it, that's it!'

On the milk farm, Vinnie timed Tory flipping an icy giant tractor tyre over and over towards a finish rope line, 'Keep going, you're beating your old time last week. That's it, don't stop!'

Stewie raised an eyebrow and nodded to himself with respect, 'He's a beast!' The paparazzi kept low behind the steel gate, continuing taking snaps of all the action.

In The Devil's Gym, Buck and Larry sat ringside, watching two fighters spar when, yet again, their attention was soon turned to Tory on the news. They looked on as they witnessed Tory jogging out of the farmhouse, along the icy path and leaping over the steel gate. The banner at the bottom of the TV read:

'*Exclusive footage of Tory's training released*'

As Buck looked on, they saw Tory flipping the giant tractor tyre with Vinnie and Stewie at his side.

'He's hungry…' muttered Larry to Buck who simply remained transfixed on the screen, nodding. Moments later, in strutted Logan dressed in his big warm coat with his gym bag coolly over his shoulder and a large Starbucks in one hand and his Twitter newsfeed on his phone in his other.

'What time you call this?'

Logan looked over his shoulder, glancing at the wall clock, 'Eleven.'

'Don't give me the big licks, smart ass. You got a big fight coming up.'

'The old retired Hobbit?'

Buck pointed the dreaded finger up at the television, 'Look! One pissed off Italian with an iron heart on a mission and with nothing to lose.'

'I'm the champ!'

'So now you're number one you wanna chill? You've finally made it to the top and now you wanna get comfortable? He's up at four! He's seven hours ahead of you already!'

'He's not just going to lie down easy,' added Larry, 'He was an animal, a beast, relentless. Small, fast, swift, nimble. A different breed to any fighter you've fought before. Don't let him tire you with more stamina.'

'Exactly,' said Buck, 'I wish your eyes burned with the same fire as his.'

'Yer, well, cool, crisp, calm waters douses flames,' finished Logan smugly.

'Cool and crisp nearly got you knocked out before.'

Logan flared up at Larry, pointing his Starbucks in his face, 'Don't…' Larry retired into his shell.

'You lose this fight, you lose all credibility.'

'Then whatta' we waitin' for?' said Logan, peeling off his winter coat and waltzing away to the changing rooms, 'Whack the heatin' up more, will yous?'

Buck simply rolled his eyes at Larry as a few chinks in their armour was established. Danger signs rattled through both of their minds; this fight wasn't going to be a pushover.

\*\*\*\*\*\*\*

Vinnie loaded weights onto the barbell resting on the bench-press machine. Tory lay down, shivering head to toe.

'The only way to survive hypothermia is to train, Tory.'

'Coach,' chattered Tory, clasping the freezing cold bar.

'Now let's see how good your muscle memory is.'

\*\*\*\*\*\*\*

Logan's tank-like arms bench pressed massive, hefty weights. Larry raised a brow at Buck, impressed by his shear strength and prowess.

\*\*\*\*\*\*\*

Meanwhile, Tory's slender arms bench-pressed a hefty weight for his size and build. His face strained red as Vinnie stood behind, spotting for Tory, gently aiding each final few reps, 'That's my boy, that's my boy. Easy…easy now.'

\*\*\*\*\*\*\*

Logan sparred with a middleweight, throwing slow, powerful punches at his swift opponent. Buck and Larry watched ringside, 'You gotta be faster, Logan. Faster! He's weaving and ducking you.'

Logan grunted in frustration, pushed the middleweight against the ropes and pounded him to the canvas. Buck sighed at Larry, 'Get me another middleweight.'

Larry nodded, watching on at the middleweight lying on the canvas—out cold, 'He's a beast.'

Buck shook his head in disappointment and crossed arms, 'Beasts are clumsy.'

*******

Amidst candlelight, Tory sparred in the ring with Stewie. Fast, swift punches connected. 'Punch, slip and block, punch, slip, block,' ordered Vinnie ringside. Tory punched, slipped, blocked Stewie's counter punch, 'Right, that's it! Like riding a bike, see? Remember what you're doing this for. Don't forget.'

The next morning, Tory headed outside to the Swingball all alone. He threw the tennis ball attached to string and punched the ball with his left. As the ball came back round, he punched it with his right. Time and time again his punches hit the ball with pinpoint accuracy as a solitary, intimate, personal game of Swingball played out.

*******

Christmas lights covered the Capital as Logan jogged over London Bridge.

*******

On the milk farm, Vinnie sprayed a white line on the grass, 'Gonna need endurance; high intensity interval training. Sprints, two-minute speed-walk. Go!' Tory and Stewie sprinted off the marker.

Later, Tory and Stewie pumped out endless press-ups.

At the rock pile, Tory, alone, ran with the barrow full of rocks.

*******

Logan pumped out endless sit-ups with Larry anchoring his feet.

*******

By the scrap yard, Tory performed sit-ups with a digger's scoop bucket on his chest.

Tory and Stewie sprinted through a stream. Tory fell, splashing flat on his face and vomited in shear exhaustion. Stewie turned around, dragged Tory to his feet and steadied him on.

*******

Logan attacked the speedball with heavy fists, 'Got anchors in your fists?' yelled Buck in his ear, 'Faster!' Logan strained and pulled out. Buck threw a sponge at Logan, 'Again!'

*******

'Vinnie ogled at Tory's fluid fists attacking the speedball with laser-guided precision, 'You got it, you still got it.' Stewie stunned, filming Tory in action from his phone.

As the sun set behind the naked winter trees in the secluded cemetery, Tory laid a white rose on the headstone and prayed as day turned to night.

In the ring and under the guise of moonlight, Tory skipped fluidly amidst the shadows in the ring.

*******

In the nice warm gym, Logan skipped swiftly on the balls of his feet, eyeing the giant wall clock and the moment the small hand reached five, he slung the rope, threw his gym bag over his monster shoulders and stomped to the door.

'Hey! Hey! Where do you think you're going?' cried out Buck and without even taking his eyes off the exit, Logan simply pointed to the wall clock. Buck shook his head in disappointment and threw down his pads.

Training over!

# White Collar

Tory and Stewie sparred under the natural blue moonlight with Vinnie scrutinizing every technique, 'Beautiful. Both of you. You got it. Faster, harder, faster! Tory, stop relenting! Attack—attack—attack! For crying out loud!'

Tory peered over his tight guard and threw a lightning fast blow square-on Stewie's chin. Stewie hit the canvas and lay sparked out. Tory panicked and hurried to his new wingman, Stewie, 'Stewie? Sorry! Shit, sorry. You okay, you okay?' Stewie remained in on his back with his eyes closed, 'Shit! Oh God!'

Vinnie leapt into the ring, opened one of Stewie's eyelids and shone a torch pen in his eyes, slapping his face in attempt to bring him round.

'What have I done?'

'It's okay, Tory, he'll be fine.'

Stewie groaned and stirred. Vinnie sat Stewie up, shining the light in his delirious eyes, 'Stewie, look at me. That's it, that's it, son. Don't move. I gotcha.'

'What happened?' asked Stewie when he suddenly puked bile onto the canvas.

'It's okay, you're okay.'

Tory stood planted. Tears streamed down his face as haunting memories of what he had caused to his brother resurfaced.

'He's okay, Tory. He's okay.'

Tory shook his head, enough was enough. He untied his gloves with his teeth, spat out his gum-shield and ducked through the ropes.

'Tory!' shouted Vinnie, knowing the fight was too close for such mental submission.

Outside, Tory rested his back against the wall and looked up at the heavens with teary eyes, 'Please God, not again, *please*,' he pleaded when the dazzling blue strobes of the ambulance caught his attention followed by Vinnie shortly after escorting Stewie out of the gym.

'What, have I been knocked out or something?' slurred Stewie, totally oblivious still as to what had happened.

'Stewie! You okay?'

'It's just precaution, Tory. You know the protocol. Don't panic.'

'Have I been knocked out or something?' asked Stewie again, forgetting that seconds ago he had just asked the same question.

Vinnie joined young Stewie in the ambulance as Tory hurried away into the darkness with only one place to be right now—next to his brother.

And here Tory sat, all alone for hours on end just…thinking about Stewie and whether he was going to be all right or not. Being knocked out was a part of boxing but Tory had a right, of course, to be so concerned.

The sound of frozen leaves crunching beneath somebody's feet soon distracted him as Vinnie stopped at his side, 'He's gonna be fine, Tory. He knows what day of the week it is now.'

Tory sighed relief, 'I shouldn't have hit him so hard.'

'It's the nature of the sport. You know this.'

'I don't know what came over me.'

'He's fine. He's still gonna fight. The question is, are *you* ready for your fight? Best get packing for the hotel. Tomorrow we recover ready for the big night.'

'I'm watching him fight; Stewie.'

'Sure. Sure thing, Tory.'

Vinnie gave Tory a lift to the hospital just in time to see Stewie and his mother signing out at reception. Stewie faced the exit doors to see Tory standing anxiously in front of him.

'Tory, what you doing here?'

'I'm sorry, Stewie,' said Tory, turning to his mother, 'I'm so sorry I hurt your boy.'

'I was hoping maybe you knocked some sense into him. All he wants to be like is you.'

'What? Don't be stupid, ma. I've been knocked out by the Saviour,' said Stewie enthusiastically, shadow boxing, 'I'm ready now.'

Tory broke a smile and embraced Stewie, 'That you are, my friend…that you are.'

Stewie's face lit up, 'Shouldn't you be in London resting for your big night?'

Tory passed Stewie two tickets to the fight, 'You serious? Tickets? For your fight?'

'Yeah, but first we got your big fight.'

'You—you're watching me fight?'

Tory nodded, 'Of course! That's what friends are for.' Stewie's face lit up ever more, 'Oh wow, really? For real?'

Yeah, really.'

Stewie faced his mother and put his arm around her, 'You hear that, ma? The infamous Salvatore De Luca's watching me fight tomorrow!'

Seeing Stewie so excited made Tory feel special, like his presence had made someone else glow, and as he turned to walk away, Stewie was still bragging to his mother:

'The Saviour, coming to watch me fight,' and whether Tory liked it or not, after everything that had happened in the past, his existence really had seemed to have saved someone's soul.

The next day, Tory was all packed and ready for London bound straight after Stewie's fight here at The Bournemouth International Centre. Masses of people queued to watch the amateur White Collar charity boxing event which had gained ever more momentum as the years passed. Inside, hundreds of spectators sat around the ring waiting for the next fight. A fighter in blue stood at his corner waiting for the red fighter to enter. 'And now, in the red corner,' continued the Master of Ceremonies, 'and weighing in at sixty-six kilograms, Stewart Stacks!' Bonnie, Robert, Vinnie, and Pat sat at a table ringside all suited and booted, clapping. Bonnie jumped to her feet, wooing Stewie and cheering him on. Stewie, in a red vest, shorts and head gear, appeared at the door with Tory at his side and headed proudly from the back of the arena towards the ring. His coach and crew clapped and waited for him in the red corner and it wasn't long until the crowd spotted their infamous local hero—Tory.

'To-ry! To-ry! To-ry!'

The shouts were electrifying. Tory smiled, waving and bowing to the crowd. He put his arm around Stewie and pointed the attention on him.

'Ste-wie! Ste-wie! Ste-wie!' cried the crowd. Stewie glowed, soaking up his five-minutes of fame.

******

Meanwhile, Kathy slept upright on the hard chair with her hand still holding Faith's hand, and in her sleep, she felt Faith's finger twitch. Kathy knew she was asleep but it felt all so real and so she woke, and when she did, she realised it wasn't a dream and that, in fact, Faith had finally come round!

'Faith? My baby…my baby! Nurse? Nurse!'

\*\*\*\*\*\*

Back at the Bournemouth International Centre, the moment the bell rang, Stewie moved in on his opponent with conviction, head tucked behind tight guard and threw swift, hard combos, chopping his opponent down blow by blow. Tory, Pat, Vinnie, Bonnie, Robert cheered and clapped at Stewie's prowess.

'That's it, punch, slip, block!' shouted Tory down on the ring. Stewie indeed punched, slipped, blocked, and countered with a stunning right hook causing his opponent in blue to drop to the canvas. The crowd erupted into a frenzy. Tory, Bonnie, Robert jumped to their feet and cheered.

'That's my boy!' muttered Tory proudly to himself.

The referee counted to ten and called the fight. Stewie leapt for joy, scanned the crowd, spotted Tory and Vinnie, and kissed his glove, sending the kiss of appreciation their way. He then laid his eyes on Bonnie and blew a kiss her way. Bonnie blew a kiss back, playing lustfully with her hair, 'Damn he's fine!'

The fun and games were over; Vinnie pointed to his watch, 'Time to go, Tory.'

Tory stood, saluted Stewie and the crowd before making his way up the stairs of the arena ready to fight the fight of his life…

# Daddy

Before the relatively long drive to London, Tory stopped off at his brother's grave one last time. He got down on one knee and said his prayers whilst Vinnie and Pat stood respectively behind.

'You ready?' asked Vinnie softly. Tory nodded and rose to his feet.

'Stay focussed,' added Vinnie, not wanting anything to hinder the upcoming fight. Pat squeezed Tory's shoulder and led him away.

In the press-room of the London O2 Arena, weighing scales stood before the Press and Officials.

'So, here we are,' started the weigh-in official, 'the day of the big fight of course. Remember this is not a championship fight and thus classed as an openweight fight, and I'm very excited to see what weight these two are going to come in at. Logan Devlin clearly going to be the dominator being a six-foot-two heavyweight, and speaking of the devil, here he is now!'

Cameras flashed as tank-like Logan entered the stage, peeled off his hoody and revealed his beef-cake torso.

'Just look at the sheer size of him!' continued the commentator as Logan stepped onto the scales for all to see.

'Sixteen,' declared the judicator, reading off the scales. 'Sixteen stone. That's two-hundred and twenty-four pounds!' said the weigh-in commentator, 'The Devil clearly not shedding mass in order to compensate for Tory's smaller yet faster fight technique and style. Tory refused to come out alongside Logan, that's how bad the hate is between the two.'

Logan snatched his hoody and left the stage.

'Now we're just waiting for Tory, probably the most anticipated fighter of the two with regards to weight and being only five-foot-eight.'

Tory stormed onto the stage with Vinnie at his side, accompanied by the flashing of cameras. He rolled off his hoody to reveal a stocky yet defined, chiselled physique.

'Wow, would you take a look at that? Tory's gained weight for this fight. I say he's touching Light Heavyweight,' said the weigh-in commentator as all silenced for the verdict from the judicator:

'Twelve-five.'

'He is! Unbelievable. That's one-hundred and seventy-five pounds which is quite substantial for Tory since he was a Middleweight weighing in around hundred and fifty-five pounds; eleven stone.'

Vinnie passed Tory his hoody and they left the stage.

'Well, there you have it. Forty-five pounds; over three stone difference. We got one hell of a fight on our hands.

That night, Faith rested on her back with Alana beside her on the bed and Kathy sitting on the chair beside when the door opened softly. Kathy swung around in panic, thinking it could be

Logan but was relieved to see Tory, hair combed and cleanly shaven poking his handsome face around the door.

'Sorry, to disturb you all,' whispered Tory, seeing the trio before him, closing the door.

'It's okay, Tory, come in,' shouted Kathy through the door.

The door opened and in crept Tory with one arm behind his back, smartly dressed and fully loaded with a humongous teddy in his hand, causing Alana's eyes to light up.

Faith broke a smile through her now faintly bruised face, 'Wow, look at you.'

'Wow, look at you, more like,' replied Tory still just as mesmerised by Faith's beauty than the first time he laid eyes on her all those years ago.

Faith chuckled, knowing that her current state was far from anything to look at, 'You're kidding, right?' Tory shook his head and gave the teddy to Alana along with the giant lolly she gave him on Halloween.

Alana's face lit up and grabbed the giant teddy and lolly.

'Aww, thanks,' uttered Faith tiredly, 'what do you say, Alana?' Alana simply hid shyly behind the teddy, 'she's just shy.'

'It's okay,' whispered Tory, revealing a big bunch of flowers and a carrier bag.

'I'll wait outside,' said Kathy, seeing her cue to leave the two to chat. Tory opened the door for Kathy before laying the flowers on the bedside table.

'What's in the bag?' asked Faith.

'Your favourite,' replied Tory, revealing a huge box of strawberry laces causing Faith to let out a drowsy chuckle. 'I even tried smuggling in fries and shake but they weren't having any of it at border patrol.' Faith giggled. Tory pointed to Alana who was now holding out the lolly to Tory for him to open the wrapper, 'Is she allowed…?' Faith nodded. Tory shakily opened the wrapper;

he was so nervous for this encounter, 'I know he hurt you, Faith. He found my gold glove and thought me and you were—'

'How…how do you know all this?'

'Everyone knows. The whole world knows. You're no longer alone, Faith.'

Faith crinkled a brow at Tory; she didn't know what was going on.

'I'm fighting him. Tomorrow night. In the ring.' Faith shook her head and recoiled, looking away from Tory, 'You're coming home—with me. In time for Christmas.'

'Home?'

'Home. Back on the farm—to begin with, then wherever you wish. There's five-hundred grand at stake.' Tory took her by the hand, 'I thought I'd lost you, Faith—twice. I don't never wanna' lose you again. If that's okay with you of course,' he nodded to Alana's presence, 'I know she's Logan's, but I'll look after her, like my own, I swear…on my brother's life.' Faith bit her lower lip in desperate attempt to stop herself from crying and shook her head slowly, 'Okay, well you can have the money, once I've helped Pat and Vinnie out anyway, and get away from him. All I care about is you whether you want to be with me or not.' On that note, Tory rose to his feet and turned around, thinking that Faith didn't want to be with him.

'I'm mean,' gasped Faith weakly, 'she's not his, Tory.'

Tory froze on the spot and slowly turned around, 'Huh?'

'She's not his.'

'But if she's not Logan's, then *whose* is she?'

An escapee tear this time rolled down her lightly bruised face.

'Do I know him?' Faith nodded. Tory wiped the tear from her face. Alana hugged Faith upon seeing her cry, 'Then it's okay. I don't care. Faith, honestly, I don't. It's not my business.' Tory turned his back on Faith and took a step to the door.

'She…she's…' Tory halted mid-step and turned around, to see teary-eyed Faith staring deep into his eyes, '*yours*, Tory.'

Tory was knocked back greater than any punch he'd ever received, 'What?'

'Alana is *your* daughter.'

'Mine? How?'

'Do I really need to teach you about the birds and the bees?'

'But why—why didn't you tell me?'

Faith pointed to Tory's head, 'you were unstable, we were over when I found out.'

'Was I that bad?'

'You lost the plot…your head. I had to, to save our unborn child from a broken home.'

Even during such an emotional moment for Tory, signs of his fire still burned through, 'You tellin' me that bastard's been bringing up my daughter?'

There he goes again.

Faith's face creased up in distress, 'Please.' Tory realised that this fragile beauty had no place for such fire and instantly extinguished the flames inside, 'I'm sorry, I'm so sorry.'

The attention soon turned to Alana who was licking her lolly and hugging her teddy. Tory gazed into his daughter's eyes for the first time and didn't know what to say or do, 'H-hello. What's your name?'

'Alana' she replied in her adorably cute voice.

'Well, hello Alana, what…what a lovely name,' although he tried, he couldn't help the tears from streaming down his creased-up face, 'She's-she's beautiful! Sure taken your good looks that's for sure.'

Faith cried tears of joy and relief as for the first time ever, she felt the family which she had always wanted, not just for her but for her daughter.

'Yours.'

'You kidding, have you seen my nose?'

Tory leant in and kissed Faith tenderly on the lips.

'Is this a dream?' asked Faith this time with a fixed grin.

'I don't know, kiss me again.'

They both smiled lustfully and chuckled when Alana stood between the two and pointed out Faith's bruised face to Tory, 'Mama!' Tory's face turned to thunder as that inextinguishable fire lit from inside, quelled by the sound of the door opening and the nurse popping her head around the door, 'Visiting time's over, I'm afraid, the girl needs rest!'

Tory nodded and rose to his feet, 'I won't ever leave you.'

'Then please don't fight him, please?'

'I must.'

Faith raised her arms out for an embrace. Tory enveloped his arms around her, bringing Alana in for a group hug.

'Don't leave us, please don't leave. He's an animal—a beast!'

Tory broke free from the group hug. His face turned serious, 'Tomorrow it ends.'

Tory lifted his daughter for the first time and held back the tears of joy, carrying her out of the room, kissing her long and hard on the cheek before passing her into Kathy's arms. Kathy didn't need to ask whether Tory had been told he's the father as the kiss said it all. Vinnie and Pat raised a brow at the sight of Tory coming out of Faith's room now equipped with a baby girl in his arms, but, once again, actions spoke louder than words and they both clapped and congratulated Tory. Tory headed along the corridor with more at stake than ever before...

Later that night, Faith slept softly and soundly when she woke to the sound of the door closing and a large harrowing shadow looming over the foot of her bed. She froze stiff, seeing Logan baring his sadistic golden grin down on her.

'Surprise!' he shouted, placing a bunch of grapes onto her bedside table. 'Grapes. Can't have you gettin' all fat on me.' He sniffed the flowers in the vase and rubbed a petal sadistically. 'Now, you didn't go around sayin' nothin', did you?' Faith shook her head slowly. 'Then what's this about Tory shoutin' his mouth to the press? Sayin' he's exposin' me.'

'I've been in a coma.'

'Do you know how damaging that is to my career? They're makin' me out the bad guy, can you believe it?' Logan reached across to Faith and whispered spitefully in her face, 'When really all along it was all *your* fault. Y'know, in other countries you'd get stoned to death for disloyalty.'

Faith trembled, receding her neck into her shoulders, 'I didn't do anything.'

'Y'know I can't stand the thought of you with another man, especially him, Tory, your ex-lover, with whom you spent the night. I'm really gonna have to shorten and tighten your leash when you get home,' he added, grabbing a strawberry lace and dangling it into his golden mouth.

'Home?'

'That nasty fall affect your memory? Yeah home, you doughnut. You didn't think you was getting rid of me that easy, did you?' He snarled his gold grin, wrapped a boot-lace around his neck as if a leash and mimicked pulling it tightly before walking himself, as if a dog, to the door. Faith watched Logan exit, slamming the door behind him. She jumped out of her skin as she lay alone in the darkness with only the beating sound of her heavy heart pounding.

# Enough

That night, back in the Dorset countryside, Marie stood alone in the kitchen stuffing a turkey, getting ready for Christmas the day after tomorrow, when the doorbell rang. At the door, she was greeted to joyous carol singers bursting into song, 'We wish you a merry Christmas, we wish you a merry Christmas, we wish you a merry Christmas and a happy new year,' continued the happy group of children and elders.

'Not tonight. Sorry,' said Marie, closing the door on the festive group, knowing this certainly wasn't going to be merry in the slightest. Nor was next year, or any years to come for that matter. She surrendered her back against the door, dismaying at the happy photos of Rocco on the wall when from upstairs came Franco's distressed cries muffling down.

'Stop it!' cried Franco.

Marie hurried up the stairs and entered the spare room to find only the light from the laptop illuminating the dark room. Franco was sitting on edge at the foot of the bed with a half bottle of whiskey in hand, and here he slumped, painfully reliving the fight between Tory and his dearest son, Rocco, as if the fight was live.

'Get off! Get off my son, you son of a bitch!' yelled Franco hoarsely to Tory fighting Rocco against the ropes, unleashing killer combination blows to body and head like an animal.

'This is unbelievable, why hasn't the ref called the fight?' shouted Jim Watt, the commentator, as Franco stood in Rocco's corner with the towel at the ready in hand to throw in.

'Franco, Rocco's trainer and father has the towel in-hand but isn't throwing it!' exclaimed Barry McGuigan.

Marie watched on as Franco jolted and reacted to each blow playing out on screen, feeling each and every punch his dearest received.

'Get outta there! Off the ropes! No, stop it, please. Stop the fight! Basta, basta!'

Marie cupped her hand over her mouth in dismay, seeing her broken husband in such a wretched state, 'Franco! Enough!'

'Stop the fight!' continued Franco, 'throw the towel, you piece of shit! Throw the damn towel!'

'A stunning left! Rocco is down!' added Jim to the sight of poor Rocco dropping to the canvas into a lifeless heap.

Marie continued watching on as right before her very eyes Franco dropped to *his* knees, as if taking the killer blow himself and bawled into a blubbering mess.

'Oh my, this doesn't look good…this does not look good.'

Marie hurried to her husband down on his knees, 'Oh Franco!'

Franco embraced Marie's waist and burrowed his face into her navel. His knuckles strained white from clasping onto her apron so tightly, 'Tell him! Tell him, Marie! Tell him to throw the towel, please!' confessed Franco as the truth rung out from Jim Watt's mouth:

'Why didn't Franco throw the towel?'

Franco bawled ever more on Jim's words. Marie caressed Franco's head whilst switching off the television and peeling the bottle of whiskey from his clutches, where together this broken couple simply consoled each other in darkness as one.

'Franco, enough,' whispered Marie, 'enough.'

'What have I done? I'm so sorry! I killed him, I killed our boy! He's buried, six-feet under in the cold, because of me, because of me…because of me. My boy. What are we going to do?'

# Fight Night

*Christmas Eve.*

Stewie and Bonnie queued amidst an infinite long line of eager spectators. A giant lit banner read: *'Everlast's Grudge Night Tour.'*

Inside the arena, Everlast logos draped all around. Spectators filled seats around the lonesome ring in the centre. Officials, promoters, managers, sponsors, reporters all sat ringside alongside the legendary commentators, Adam Smith and Johnny Nelson.

'Well, it's finally here,' shouted Adam through the mic over the hustle and bustle of the crowd, 'The infamous Grudge Match Tour has touched down here in the UK's most prestigious home of boxing. A very good evening to you all and merry Christmas... and welcome to London's O2 Arena for tonight's openweight grudge match brought to you by Everlast and Sky Sports. I'm Adam Smith and with me tonight, the one and only Johnny

Nelson.' Johnny nodded at Adam and grinned into the camera, 'A very good evening, and what a line up we have. Can you believe we're seeing The Devil against The Saviour in an openweight bout, Adam?'

'I know, Johnny, who would ever have imagined it. I'm so excited I can hardly contain myself,

'I just want these preliminary fights to be over with and cut right to the chase.'

Franco and Marie shimmied past seated spectators close to the front and sat at their designated seats. Marie sat on edge, fanning her face with her program. Franco broke an assuring smile at Marie and held her hand.

Faith sat up in her hospital bed, watching the fight on her iPad with Alana sleeping beside her and with Kathy at her side, 'Stop shaking, baby,' said Kathy to Faith.

'I can't help it, mother,' replied Faith with strawberry laces hanging from her mouth.

In Logan's changing room, cheers from the crowd muffled through the door. Buck taped up Logan's beastly fists whilst Larry rubbed Vaseline across Logan's brow.

Inside Tory's changing room, Vinnie taped up Tory's shaky, battered and deformed fists, 'Hold still, will ya?' said Vinnie to Tory, 'Listen to me, you got this. Tire him out. Keep moving. Let him work, waste punches, get him frustrated, use it against him. You got four rounds—max, I'd say, before you're running on fumes.'

'Heart.'

'Say what?'

'Before I'm running on heart.'

'That's right—that's right—heart!' Pat entered, suited and booted for the occasion and held the door open for Tory causing the vacuum of cheers to rush through, coating Tory head to toe with an electrifying sense of goose bumps.

'We're up!' announced Pat, taking a swig from his hipflask as Michael Buffer, the master of ceremonies could be heard from in the ring.

'Laaaaaadies and gentlemen...'

Tory fixated on the door as the true reality of the moment sank in. Vinnie slapped Tory's cheeks to keep him focussed, 'Float like a butterfly, sting like a bee.' Tory took a long deep breath and exhaled long and slow; he had never felt this nervous before.

In the main arena, Michael Buffer paced in the ring, firing up the sell-out crowd, '...Here is the moment you've all been waiting for...'

'Well, this is it. Crunch time,' said Adam to Johnny and the millions of viewers at home as Michael continued:

'... And now, for tonight's main event brought to you by Everlast and Sky Sports. And introducing, in the red corner, the one and only and Britain's number one Heavyweight champion, Logaaaaaaaaan 'the Devil' Devlinnnnnn!!!'

A majority of boos erupted and rang out throughout the arena. Adam and Johnny scanned the booing crowd.

'An eruption of boos for Logan. I'd say eighty percent of spectators are gunning for Tory, Johnny.'

'I agree! And they say there's no such thing as bad publicity.'

Strobe lights flashed and heavy rock played through the speakers. Smoke caused a silhouette of Logan's monstrous presence hopping on the spot ready to walk on.

'Here's The Devil now! He didn't cut any weight for Tory.'

On his cue, Logan stormed past the rowdy crowd with a hard, stone-cold composure.

'Just look at him,' said Johnny.

'I'm quivering just looking at him, Johnny.'

'Me too, Adam.'

Kathy entered Faith's room loaded with coffee to see Faith looking away from her iPad; she couldn't bear to look at him; the man she once loved and sought protection from.

Larry peeled off Logan's devil embroidered silky robe to reveal Logan's tank-like frame.

Logan clambered into the ring, hopping on the spot.

'He's still a tank,' uttered Adam over the Master of Ceremonies.

'And coming to you from the blue corner, resurrected from the dead and weighing in at one- hundred and seventy-five pounds, Salvatore 'The Saviour' De Lucaaaaaa!!!'

The crowd roared, cheered, and whistled, looking eagerly back at where Tory would be walking out from.

'Just listen to that response, Adam!'

Spotlights and strobes illuminated the waving crowd when the haunting tone of the piano played out though the speakers.

'I recognise this song, Johnny.'

'It's what his brother always walked out to; Ludovico Einaudi.'

On his cue, Tory stormed along the aisle in only his shorts, with a thousand-yard stare and a perfectly toned physique.

'Here's Tory now, Johnny, putting on just over a stone-and-a-half for this fight.'

'Just look at that definition! Never seen him so chiselled.'

'Unbelievable what a matter of months can do to you.'

Stewie and Bonnie leapt off their seats, cheering and whistling.

Faith cheered and wooed. Kathy grabbed Alana's hands and clapped for her.

'Oh my God, mum, his body, look at his body!' Kathy raised a brow at the impressive sight of Tory.

In Logan's corner, Larry shoved in Logan's black gum-shield whilst Logan simply stared past Buck and fixated on the spotlight on Tory, 'Where is he? Where is he?'

'Stay calm. Cool, calm waters, remember?'

The moment Tory ducked through the ropes, Logan headed straight for him like a Lion preying on a gazelle, I'm gonna kill you!

You hear? *Kill* you!'

Tory cast his thousand-yard stare on Logan, rolling his neck coolly and calmly, leaving Larry and Buck to hold psychotic Logan back.

'Save it for the ring—the ring!' stressed Larry, tugging Logan with all his might back to his corner but Logan simply pushed Larry with his free hand, sending him onto the canvas.

'Get your vile hands off me! Let me at him!' spat Logan.

Adam and Johnny watched on ringside with shear disbelief.

'This is more than a grudge. This is shear hate, Johnny!'

'And there goes The Devil again, pushing people around like a bully!'

The crowd cheered to show being put on for them. Vinnie turned Tory to his corner and placed in his gum shield.

'He really doesn't like you.'

'I hate him more.'

'Now, you got this! Stay focussed. Run circles round him.' Vinnie shadow-boxed, 'One-two-out, one two-out, just like we rehearsed, okay?' Vinnie sprayed water in Tory's face to keep him fresh and alert, 'It's all down to you. Remember why you're here. Keep pinching yourself.'

Pat clambered up onto the ring and talked over the ropes, 'How you feeling?'

'Alive.'

Pat beamed a smile, took a swig from his hipflask and patted Tory's shoulder, 'That's my boy. Proud of you, laddy.'

Vinnie placed his hand lovingly against Tory's cheek, 'Put all your rage into this page. You got this.' Tory nodded and turned to face the ring. Vinnie ducked through the ropes, leaving Tory now alone in the ring with The Devil.

The referee pointed Tory and Logan to the ring's centre. Logan towered over Tory and snarled through his black gum-shield. Tory stared up at Logan with a murderous look.

'I Tweeted first round,' grimaced Logan as the ref stood between the two.

'I want a clean, fair fight. No illegal blows. Now, shake hands.'

'Tonight, she comes home with me.'

'Tonight, you come home in a box like your brother.'

Tory raged, and jostled with the referee to get at him.

Adam recoiled from his chair as if the fight was headed his way, 'I don't know what The Devil has just said, Johnny, but it's clearly enraged the Saviour!'

'Something about returning home in a box just like his brother, or something, Adam, is what I caught.'

'Well, that's just below the belt. There's just no need for that.'

Logan and Tory made their way to their individual corners whilst Adam and Johnny could be seen commentating through the ropes.

'Surprise—surprise. No handshake, Johnny.'

The referee made his way to the centre of the ring, glanced over at Logan, Tory, the judges:

'Let's get it on!'

Ding—ding! And on the sound of the bell, it was fight on.

The crowd roared into action. Marie prayed up at the heavens and crossed herself.

Tory raised his guard to Southpaw.

'Here it is, the moment we've all been waiting for; The Devil versus The Saviour.'

Logan ran in, throwing heavy jabs, trying to get Tory against the ropes to unleash a beating, but Tory weaved and dodged with his immaculate footwork. Logan swung savage hooks with such velocity that he stumbled over his own feet whilst Tory remained composed, skipping on the balls of his feet, weaving and ducking every punch.

'Come on!' shouted Logan, beckoning Tory with a glove.

Adam scrutinised the situation, 'Logan getting frustrated as he can't land a shot.'

'He'll be exhausted in no time if he keeps wasting blows like that,' added Johnny.

Tory darted in with one-two combos and got out in a flash.

'Tory gets in with a flash combo and straight out of the danger zone.'

'Remarkable, Adam.'

Logan picked his moment, throwing a haymaker but missed, leaving himself open to attack. Tory capitalized and threw a mighty left to the ribs.

Logan stumbled back and reached for his side in pain.

'Tweet that!' shouted Tory to Logan over the cheering crowd.

Vinnie pounded the edge of ring with his palms, 'That's it!' Logan shrugged off the blow and recomposed himself to see Tory beckoning him with his gloves. Being like red rag to a bull, Logan charged in, fist raised. Tory waited for the right moment, pivoted around Logan like a matador and leapt forward, throwing a beautiful left. Logan held his right cheek, turned around 'bull-like' and charged in again. This time, Tory pivoted out of the way and released a right hook.

Logan stumbled back, holding his left cheek.

'Tory playing Logan like some matador,' said Adam.

Buck shouted through the ring, 'Concentrate! Cool, calm waters!' Logan moved in with more conviction, feinted an obvious right with throwing a left haymaker clean on Tory's face, dropping Tory to the canvas in one punch.

Vinnie and Pat cringed ringside.

Faith yelled and Kathy wailed upon seeing Tory go down. Alana stirred and woke, 'Sorry, Laney! Mum, he's down—he's down!'

Stewie and Bonnie cringed, sinking their head into hands. Marie covered her eyes with her hands, 'I can't watch this, Franco!'

Franco rested his hand on her leg, 'He'll recover, he's a De Luca.'

Buck high-fived Larry, 'That's changed the game.'

The referee towered over Tory and begun the count leaving Logan smirking behind him.

'Three...four...five...'

Vinnie rattled the lower rope, 'Up!'

The lights from the arena felt blinding to Tory as they blurred and spun. The crowd's discord reaction distorted in his head and so did the referee's count suddenly tuning in like some radio station, '...six...' Tory shrugged himself onto his side and staggered to his wobbly feet before dropping down again onto his knees where he crawled, on all fours, to the ropes all the while blinking heavily.

'He's truly rattled!' shouted Adam.

'Yeah, I don't think he's going to recover from that one.'

Tory grabbed the bottom rope and pulled himself up, but his wobbly Bambi legs sent him down onto the canvas.

'Tory really looking like he's in trouble here.'

Tory grabbed the bottom rope again and heaved with all his might.

'Seven...eight...'

'Up! Up! Up!' barked Vinnie hoarsely.

Tory stood and swayed like a boat on choppy waters much to the crowd's content. Stewie and Bonnie joined in, cheering and clapping Tory on.

The Referee held Tory's hands out in front of him and scrutinized his eyes when the end of round bell rung. The Referee called a halt to the round.

Tory staggered to The Devil's corner, but Logan soon sent him in the right direction by barging him out of the way, sending Tory back to the canvas.

'Get to your own corner!'

Boos erupted from the crowd aimed at Logan.

Tory clambered back to his feet. Vinnie ducked through the ropes and escorted Tory to his corner, sitting him down on the small stool, 'What day is it?'

'I'm okay—I'm okay!' slurred Tory, guzzling water from the water bottle in Pat's hand at a rate of knots.

Logan acted coolly on his stool yet panting for breath from all that run around. Buck gave the orders whilst Larry squirted water into Logan's mouth.

'That's better! Use your strength against him. He's too fast for you. He's been out the game too long; he'll tire in later rounds then take him out.'

Logan spat a mouthful of water into the bucket, 'I'm taking him out now! Gonna prove to the world it was a cheap-shot.'

Vinnie pressed a steal dolly against Tory's swelling eye. 'Don't let him in. Keep moving. One-two out. One-two out!' Tory nodded, his eyes rolled back and his head dropped back. 'Tory, stay with me now—stay with me!'

Ding—ding sounded the bell for round two. The hungry crowd cheered the two fighters rising to their feet.

'Round two, and Tory still looking a little wobbly and swollen under that right eye, Johnny.'

'Yes, another blow like that from the Devil and it's all over.' Logan and Tory fought like warriors.

Logan threw hefty lefts and rights with Tory weaving and ducking.

Logan capitalised on his long reach, unleashing explosive jabs into Tory risen guard, trying to break through. Tory parried a jab downwardly and counter-jabbed a left to Logan's face. The crowd erupted into a frenzy.

'A beautiful counter punch!' shouted Adam watching Tory get out of there in a flash.

'You see, that's why parrying is a superior defensive move

than simply blocking. It offers more protection while creating better counter opportunities using your opponent's energy,' explained Johnny over the bell's ding for the end of round two.

'A better round from Tory,' he added.

'Yeah, I have him down for that round; The Saviour.' Buck sat Logan on the stool and told him how it is whilst Larry continued applying Vaseline to his face, 'You're not fast enough! You gotta keep moving!'

In Tory's corner, Vinnie pressed a steel dolly against Tory's swollen eye, 'That's better. You see? You keep parrying and counter punching like that you'll have him. There's nowhere for him to go.'

'He's got a meat-head. I'm not affecting him.'

'You punch an oak tree a thousand times in a thousand different places and what's going to happen?'

'Nothing.'

Nothing, right! But if you punch it thousand times in the same place what's going to happen? You're gonna bring that fucker down. Keep chopping. Chop—chop—chop!' The bell dinged for round three, 'Vary your combos. Chop the body. Okay? Now go do it.' Tory nodded, rising to his feet.

'Round three,' announced Adam.

Johnny scrutinized Tory's eye through the ropes.

'Tory's swollen eye certainly looks like it's in for the night; the destruction that can be caused from a devastating single blow.'

Tory weaved and ducked Logan's killer blows.

'Tory straight back to business. Weaving and ducking, tiring the Devil out.'

Logan stepped in and jabbed but Tory sideway parried this time, throwing Logan's punch and body weight over his shoulder much to Johnny's delight.

A sideways parry! Logan's gone flying through, missing entirely and leaving his body open.'

Tory took advantage, countering with body and face combos.

'Tory now taking advantage with explosive left and right combos all over The Devil!'

The crowd rose and cheered, seeing Tory having Logan against the ropes.

'Get out! Get outta there!' cried Buck.

'Logan seems like he doesn't know where to block.'

'Logan's going to go down if he doesn't get outta there!'

Tory chopped and chopped at Logan and a swift left to the side sent him down on his knees.

The crowd burst into an electrifying frenzy.

'He's down! The Devil is down and the referee is counting!'

'Two...three...four...'

Stewie leapt to his feet, waving a fist, going ballistic. 'He's down! Get in there my son!'

Faith screamed, hugging Kathy, 'I don't believe it!'

Logan clambered to one knee.

'Five...six...'

Logan stood sheepishly yet shrugged the severity of the moment off to the scrutinizing referee.

Ding—ding sounded the bell. Adam wiped sweat from his brow, 'Logan this time saved by the bell.'

'Yeah, again, he's got to move out quicker than that or he's going to get landed, Adam.'

'My God, I'm sweating here just watching. I'm actually sweating.'

Larry sponged Logan's sore ribs. Buck fed the water bottle to Logan, 'You're falling into his trap. He's out-boxing you. You run the show, you lead this dance. He's tiring. Make him waste blows hitting your guard. You're the champ! He's a dwarf compared to you. Now show the world what you're made of and let's go home.'

Tory sat on his stool, panting for air allowing Vinnie to apply Vaseline to his face, 'Beautiful, beautiful. Round four, Tory. More of the same. Keep running circles around him!'

Ding—ding!

Tory and Logan rose off their stools.

'Round four.'

More of the same; Tory released fast, powerful punches.

Logan hid behind his tightly tucked guard, absorbing every blow.

'Don't waste shots!' shouted Vinnie through the ropes.

'Tory now looking he can't get inside,' commented Johnny, looking on at Tory's punches hitting Logan's guard over and over.

'And tiring,' added Adam.

'Tactical strategy here from The Devil.'

The bell dinged for the end of round 4.

Tory dragged his heels to his corner. 'A strategic defensive round there by the Devil. Hardly threw a punch and just allowed the Saviour to waste punches,' said Adam to Johnny. 'And it worked. Tory dragging his heels to his corner now.'

Vinnie plonked gasping Tory onto the stool, 'How you feeling?'

'Tired! So…tired!'

'Deep breaths. Deep breaths. Round five, Tory. You're in unchartered waters from here now. Conserve your energy. Don't waste blows.'

Ding—ding!

Vinnie helped Tory onto his feet.

Tory raised his guard, feeling like he was carrying a ship's anchor.

'Tory can barely raise his arms,' said Johnny to Adam. Straight off, Logan punched Tory into the ropes, throwing combinations. Tory tucked his chin behind his tight guard and took the hefty blows, leaving Logan to chop and chop away at Tory. Savage blows broke through Tory's guard, pounding his body and face.

'Tory really looking rattled now.'

'He can barely defend himself and surely the referee won't have much more of this punishment.'

Logan got in tight to Tory and made the mistake of his life:

'Told you you'd be joining your brother!'

Tory roared, lifted mighty Logan, swivelled him around and pinned him against the ropes and unleashed true hell.

'Tory seeming to have found a new lease of life!' shouted Adam, witnessing swift, killer blows pounding Logan's body and face, rattling Logan. Logan pushed Tory away but Tory pushed Logan back into the ropes.

'This is insanity! Out of hand!' added Johnny, watching on at Tory's left and rights chopping Logan down.

'His sweet spot!' roared Vinnie, 'Aim for the sweet spot!'

Tory teed it up, hitting the ribs—kidneys—face—face—kidneys—ribs. Logan shrieked, pushed Tory away, lowering his guard to clutch his side in pain and with this golden opportunity, Tory propelled forward, left fist drawn, and released a haymaker clean on Logan's square jaw. Logan crashed against the corner post and clutched the rope for dear life. His legs buckled in and wobbled.

'That's the sweet spot!' roared Vinnie.

'And now it's the Devil who's in trouble!'

'And looking very wobbly on his feet, Adam!'

Tory pushed Logan into the corner and unleashed five-punch combos to the face and body; pah—pah—pah—pah—pah!

Logan's guard confused, not knowing where to block.

'Tory has Logan in the corner!'

'He's going to do it!'

'Keep chopping!' yelled Vinnie.

'Go on, Laddy!' spurred Pat.

Faith squealed in delight, not wanting to wake Alana, 'Go on, yes—yes—yes!'

Tory punched Logan relentlessly.

A beautiful left hook to the jaw sent Logan's gum-shield flying.

'There goes the Devil's gum- shield!'

Tory wound back his left fist ready for the killer blow just as the referee shimmied between the two to peel the two away, and amidst all the explosive action, Tory released his killer left, burying it straight into the side of the *referee's* head, sending him onto the canvas, causing Logan to stagger backwards out of the way and sway deliriously.

'Sorry!' yelled Tory as instantly he remembered doing the same to his brother. Harrowing memories resurfaced from the dark depths of his guilt stricken soul.

'The referee is down! He's been caught by a hefty blow from Tory!'

'That punch was for Logan and I think it would've been the end game for The Devil!'

Tory recoiled, turned his stricken face away out to the crowd and closed his eyes in dismay as the haunting flashbacks continued to surface, leaving Logan to recompose himself.

'Tory's froze!'

Stewie faced Bonnie in disbelief, 'What's he doing?' Bonnie simply shrugged.

Faith gasped behind her hands, 'Oh no! N—n—no!'

Pat and Vinnie stood dumbfounded, 'What's he doing, Vinnie?'

'He's froze, why's he froze? Take him! Now—now—now!' Logan snarled through his golden mouth, grinned menacingly and slowly moved in on Tory.

The referee clambered onto his knees, picked up Logan's gum-shield and grabbed the bottom rope to heave himself off the canvas.

Tory peeped through one eye down on the referee to see Rocco's face replace the referee's face!

'No…' he whispered to himself, grabbing his head to rid his hallucinations and so ignoring Vinnie's shouts to end Logan now.

Tory keeled over the ropes, shaking his head.

Vinnie spotted Logan moving in and grabbed the towel ready to throw it in. 'Vinnie has the towel in hand! He's going to end it.'

The Referee stood on wobbly legs and tried inserting Logan's gum-shield but Logan whacked the gum-shield out of the Referee's hand, continuing to limp towards Tory.

'Turn around!' roared Vinnie through the ropes, scrunching the towel tightly into a ball.

Marie squirmed, hiding behind her hands, 'Stop it! Call the fight! Please! Please Franco, do something!'

Franco stood and stormed ringside, 'Throw the towel!'

Stewie covered his eyes, 'Don't throw it!' Johnny spotted Franco pass behind him and nudged Adam, 'Is that Tory's father who's just passed us, Adam?'

'I think it was, you know, Johnny.'

Tory spotted Franco below him at his corner jostling with Vinnie for the towel with Pat standing between the two in desperate attempt to split them up.

'Da?' uttered Tory, completely stunned and thinking he was again hallucinating. Logan capitalised and buried a right haymaker into Tory's face.

Tory hit the canvas like a sack of potatoes. Blood poured from under his good eye.

'Tory's down and cut!'

'Cut real bad just under his good eye, indeed, Adam!'

Bonnie buried her face into Stewie's arm, 'No! I can't watch!'

Faith pulled her bed sheets over her head, 'I can't watch, mother!'

'The tides have changed,' declared Adam, 'This isn't looking good for The Saviour.'

Vinnie shouted through the ropes to Tory only feet away, 'Get up!' but through Tory's eyes, Franco stood amidst the blurry, spinning crowd.

Tory rolled onto his front, onto his knees and sobbed, 'Da?'

'Come on, son. Enough is enough,' uttered Franco to his son.

Marie leapt to her feet and hurried ringside.

Tory reached through the ropes for his father with blood gushing from his eye onto the canvas, 'Da! I'm sorry. I'm so—so sorry! P—please...forgive me,' he whimpered as the referee continued the count.

'Five...six...'

Franco extended his arm through the ropes and held Tory's hand.

The crowd silenced in shock and awe.

'Tory seeming to be more focussed on reconciling with his father than the fight, Johnny.'

Franco pointed up, 'It wasn't your fault. Come on, son, let's go home.'

Tory shook his head with sorrow.

Vinnie slammed his hands onto the canvas, 'Tory, get up! You can do it. Think how far you've come. You're not going back to the farm—there is no farm. It's make or break. Do it for him, do your *brother* proud.'

Tory instinctively grabbed the middle rope, roared and heaved with all his might, love, and heart.

'Seven...eight...'

Tory stood to his feet and swayed causing the entire arena to cheer and clap, 'To-ry—To-ry—To-ry!'

'I don't believe it, Adam'

'Heart. You can't teach it, Johnny, as you know.'

Tory's streaming tears diluted the pouring blood from his eye, 'I'm so sorry,' he gasped through bated breath.

The referee scrutinized Tory and allowed the fight to go on.

'The referee taking a good look at Tory and is allowing the

fight to go on, and I really don't know whether he should.'

'Of, course he shouldn't, it's just a sport. Remember what happened to Rocco De Luca, his very own brother, when he tragically stopped breathing for five-minutes and was comatose for eighteen months.'

Logan raised a brow at Tory—a slight glimmer of respect, before raising his guard and moving in.

Tory fell into a cathartic moment. He scanned the hungry crowd; Glanced up at the spotlights.

Sponsors draped every corner.

Hungry press swarmed ringside as cameras flashed in his eyes.

Commentators and judges fixated on him, muttering to one another.

Meanwhile, Logan loomed closer, drawing back an iron fist.

Tory double-glanced to see Marie hurrying past the commentators and judges. He followed her through swollen, bloody eyes, 'Ma?'

Logan wound back the killer blow.

'Tory, behind—behind you!'

Faith peeped through the sheets, 'What's he doing? Behind you!'

Through Tory's eyes, the crowd recoiled and cringed with dread, living out the pending deadly blow coming his way as they pointed to the looming danger behind him.

Tory looked down into Marie's teary stricken eyes as he felt Logan's shadow looming over him.

The arena silenced.

Logan released the killer blow.

Tory watched his mother brace herself, wince, and shout 'No.'

Tory spun on sixpence and stepped up to Logan.

Marie jolted in shock and awe;

What happened?

The arena gasped as Logan's swollen eyes rolled back before

by his monstrous body slid down Tory's perfect left uppercut crashing to the canvas.

Kathy shouted and clapped, causing Alana to jump out of her skin and wake and Faith to peer over her sheets to see The Devil, the man she once considered her saviour, now out cold on the canvas. She cheered and clapped.

The crowd grew ecstatic. Stewie and Bonnie roared, looked lustfully into each other's eyes, and kissed passionately.

Vinnie and Franco leapt for joy whilst Pat embraced a very overwhelmed Marie.

'Logan is down for the second time. A perfect left uppercut has rattled Logan's glass jaw!'

Logan fits and spasms uncontrollably on the canvas surrounded by bloody gold teeth in which Tory had promised to wipe off his face.

Tory lowered his guard, knowing the fight was over. The crowd gasped and stood on the balls of their feet to get a look in at what was going on.

The Referee called the fight and dropped to his knees beside Logan, signalling for the medics who shortly after leapt through the ropes to tend to Logan.

'Logan appears to be in a bad state, Adam.'

'History has tragically repeated itself as medics frantically hurry to Logan's aid.'

Vinnie faced Franco and awed, 'Well, I'll be...'

Tory lowered his gaze.

Franco leapt through the ropes, placed the towel around Tory and embraced him, 'Well done, son.' Tory deflated into his father's loving arms and sobbed.

Vinnie pulled Marie up into the ring so she could finally join her son and embrace him. She ran to her only son and threw her arms around him, 'Oh, Tory! I've missed you so much!'

'I'm sorry. I'm so sorry.'

'It wasn't your fault, son. We'll work it out—we'll work it out.' assured Franco.

The assuring words from his father releasing Tory from his life sentence of blame made Tory cry ever more so, and with an overwhelming sudden sense of urgency:

'Come on, I've got somebody to show you.'

Franco and Marie crinkled a brow at one another before guiding Tory though the ropes and onto terra firma to be welcomed by Vinnie and Pat's warm embrace.

'The Saviour,' said Vinnie with a beaming proud smile.

'Well done, my laddy,' added Pat, 'Y'nearly had me ol' cockles pickled for a wee moment, you did.'

Tory broke a smile and without further ado, the five headed away from the ring with no post fight interview or anything. Tory looked back one last time to see medics urgently carrying Logan away in a stretcher.

# Rekindled

Faith and Kathy watched the iPad; the aftermath of the fight with Alana asleep on the bed. They couldn't believe the fight they had just witnessed as Adam and Johnny's final commentary spoke out:

'Can you believe the fight we've just witnessed, Johnny?'

'You know what, Adam, I don't think I can.'

The door opened slowly. Faith and Kathy fixated on the unexpected guests as Tory's excited hushes were heard,

'Shush, come on, it's a surprise,' whispered Tory, holding the door open for Marie, Franco, Vinnie and Pat to creep on through, 'Hello, princess. You got a minute?'

Faith wiped a happy tear, holding her arms out to Tory for a hug, and the moment she felt the warm embrace of her true love, she couldn't help but sob happy tears of joy and relief, 'I've got a lifetime. Oh, Tory, The Saviour. My saviour! I love you.'

'I love you more.'

Tory stepped aside, pointed at little Alana sleeping tightly in her pyjamas, 'Ma? Da? Meet Alana…your granddaughter…'

'What? How?' whispered Marie, dumbfounded.

'Do I really need to teach you the birds and the bees?'

'Oh my, she's beautiful!'

'She takes after her mother,' said Tory, winking at Faith.

'Oh, Tory, get outta here, you charmer,' chuckled Faith.

'You have a family?' asked Franco in shear disbelief.

'We, da, we,' replied Tory with a beaming smile.

Tory embraced his father, his mother, and forming as a queue, they moved onto Faith, hugging and reconciling with her..

Tory stood beside Vinnie and Pat, checking his watch, 'Beer?'

'Thought you'd never ask,' whispered Vinnie.

Pat shook his empty hip flask, 'Amen to that.'

Over the brief silence, the voice of Adam Smith and Johnny Nelson signed out of the night's big event, 'Well, from everyone here at the O2 Arena and Sky Sports, a very Merry Christmas and Happy New Year. The only question is, will we ever see The Saviour step back in the ring or is it all over for good?'

All eyes in the room focussed on Tory for an answer. Tory pondered for a brief moment, looked on at his new family and his new beginnings, 'It's ciao for now.'

******

A white butterfly fluttered high above the snow blanketed vast fields and cottages of the Dorset countryside.

The butterfly fluttered over Rocco's grave.

It fluttered over the Stinging Butterfly gym.

It fluttered over the bare oak tree.

It fluttered over the milk farm and descended towards the farmhouse. The foreclosure sign lay on the snow as the living room window loomed closer and closer where festive cheers and celebrations could soon be heard.

'More wine?' asked the cheery voice of Marie.

'Wine? What about my home brewed tipple?' asked Pat's voice.

'I think Pat needs water,' said Tory's merry voice.

'Or fresh air,' chuckled Faith.

'Yeah, before he's asleep face-down in his lunch,' added Tory to the sound of laughter.

The butterfly fluttered against the living room window to see inside Pat, Tory, Faith, Marie, Franco, Vinnie, Alana all sitting around a huge table with party hats on.

Franco liked where Pat was coming from, 'The stronger stuff sounds good to me!'

Pat winked proudly at Franco, 'A man who knows his stuff. Will blow your cockles off!'

Faith cut Alana's dinner into tiny pieces and rolled her eyes at Pat's tongue.

'Pat!' said Vinnie, nodding to young Alana's presence.

'What? It's true, I tell you.' Alana pointed at Pat; his rosy red cheeks, his giant white beard causing all to silence in anticipation to what was to come, 'Santa!'

Laughter erupted around the table. Pat laughed all jolly—just like Santa would, raising his glass, and through his rosy cheeks and white bushy beard announced, 'Merry Christmas!'

The happy family playing out wished one another a merry Christmas.

Tory lowered his gaze for a moment, remembering his dearest brother whom he missed so much and was filled with sorrow.

Faith gasped at the window, nudging Tory and nodding to the white butterfly at the window.

Tory glowed at the sight and raised his glass to the butterfly:

'Ti amo, my brother.'

Faith nestled into Tory's side and squeezed him tightly, as their new life together as one big family started today.

The end

# ABOUT THE AUTHOR

Jo-Lee is an author from Dorset, England. Typically specialising in writing his own screenplays, he ventured forth adapting his own scripts into novels in order to gain more exposure to his work. His ethos is to educate, entertain, empower, and enlighten his readers through the power of story.

# MORE BOOKS FROM THE AUTHOR

## THE LIGHTBRINGER (Sci-fi)

Set inside the recently widowed Floyd Loveless, a potentially toxic B-cell on the run from the body's defences spots an evil plotting to attack Floyd's heart and vanquish its remaining Light…

## BADPAW (Fire Edition)

As the devastating wildfires rage through Australia, a lonely little girl hurries to nurse an injured dingo pup back to health before her dingo hating rancher father finds out her secret friendship...

## BADPAW (Ice Edition)

Set in the Northern Rockies, a lonely little girl hurries to nurse an injured wolf pup back to health before her wolf hating rancher father finds out her secret friendship…

## MOONCHILD (Fantasy, coming 2020)

An orphaned little girl with special traits escapes execution to find a magical world in peril only she can save…

Printed in Great Britain
by Amazon